HER OWN HERO

Jenn Sadai

Cathy
I know there
is a hero in
you!
Believe in yourself
Always
Jenn Sadai

JCP
Jan-Carol
Publishing, Inc
"every story needs a book"

Her Own Hero
Jenn Sadai

Published February 2017
Little Creek Books
Imprint of Jan-Carol Publishing, Inc

Front Cover Design: Kim Harrison
Book Design: Tara Sizemore

ISBN: 978-1-945619-15-1
Library of Congress Control Number: 2017936291

You may contact the publisher:
Jan-Carol Publishing, Inc
PO Box 701
Johnson City, TN 37605
publisher@jancarolpublishing.com
jancarolpublishing.com

This story is dedicated to every hero. To anyone who has ever wanted to give up, but found the strength to keep going. To those who overcome challenge after challenge without losing their fighting spirit. To every person who has felt like they couldn't possibly endure anymore, and yet they did. Thank you for being your own hero. Your life was worth saving.

Letter to the Reader

We have all experienced that life shattering moment that we think will break us. Sometimes it's after a week or month or year of feeling like things couldn't possibly get worse, and then they suddenly do. It feels like the weight of the world keeps pushing you farther and farther down. You begin to feel hopeless and useless, unsure if you'll ever rise back up again.

When everything starts to fall apart, we pray for a hero to rush in and save us. We struggle and panic, wondering if we have what it takes to survive. We make attempt after attempt to regain solid ground, until one day we do. Suddenly a voice rises from within, urging us to keep fighting. We miraculously find the inner strength to carry on. Somehow, someway, we figure out how to save ourselves.

I wrote this story to remind every woman that she has the ability to be her own hero. There's a resilient fighter deep inside who has what it takes to make it through anything life throws at you. Trust that you have the power to be your own hero.

With love always,

Jenn Sadai

FOREWORD

By Ms. Camay

Everyone in the world has experienced some level of unexpected turmoil in their life. It could have happened when they were very young or it could have happened when they were well into their adult life. No matter what the experience was, I am certain there was a time when you thought to yourself, *I am not going to survive this.*

Jenn Sadai is a woman who has, in fact, experienced her own personal turmoil. She struggled with her own self-esteem, self-worth and value of herself and her physical appearance so badly, that it almost cost her life. One day she finally realized just how much she meant to herself. She is gifted in her ability to share stories and personal testimonies that reach out to other people who are, or who have, experienced similar circumstances and empower them to get through it. As an international best-selling author myself, I understand the platform of writing, while respecting the power that writing contains.

We live in a world today that is full of negativity that is plastered all over social media and the news. We are shown every day just how difficult it is to live. We see images in magazines and on television that send the message, "this is how you are supposed to look" or "this is how much you are supposed to weigh" or "this is where you should own a home" or "women are simply sexual objects" or "there are no good men in the world" or "there are no good women in the world." We are constantly fed with dysfunctional messages that we internalize, which build our belief systems that bind us for life. We, as women, were made to create life, to give life and to nurture life and where we lead, others will follow.

As a coach and mentor in pageantry, I worked with women who were operating from an insecure, introverted space. They were empowered to put their fears behind them and get up on a stage representing their greatness, being completely transformed, never to be the same. It is amazing to watch, especially when they win a national title! The women I coached came from all walks of life and the only reason I am able to celebrate these women is because, together, we were able to support and encourage each other through our own personal testimonies. This is precisely what you can expect to get from reading this book.

I could not put this book down! I stayed up until 2:00 am two days in a row to complete this short read. It was full of suspense and excitement on every page, keeping me focused on one thing, "How in the world is she going to survive this?" I mean, just when I thought one situation was going to work itself out, another circumstance presented itself which made survival seem impossible. Each time I read one of Jenn's books, my heart is filled with love, compassion, grace, forgiveness and joy, and although I may have not experienced what she specifically wrote about, I can relate the experience to one of my own, and find the same strength and courage that Jenn used to get through what she has gone through. If you are going through something in your life right now and you cannot see the light at the end of the tunnel, this book will give you the encouragement you need to turn on your own spotlight and be your own hero! You got this, Kings and Queens!

Ms. Camay is an International Best-Selling Author, Humanitarian Award Recipient, Lifetime Titleholder in Pageantry, and Legal Professional. Visit her online at www.mscamay.com.

ACKNOWLEDGMENTS

Special thanks to Diane Awram for her expertise and advice. Forever grateful to Kim Harrison and Jan-Carol Publishing, Inc. for creating another amazing book cover. Always appreciative of the support I receive from Rob Sadai, Christine Boakes, Liz Cormier, Jeremy Boakes, Shawna Boakes, Rahel Levesque, Deb Birchard, Bill Birchard, Michelle White, Sarah Pinsonneault, Kim Chapieski, Louise Smith, April Wood and Camay McClure. I'm truly blessed to have each of you in my life.

Born into a Lesser Life

I'm not really surprised that I ended up in jail.

I'm thoroughly shocked about the circumstances that led to my arrest, but I knew at a young age that there was a good chance I'd end up behind bars. It wasn't until recently that I could even imagine having a normal life as a law-abiding citizen. I used to believe my path in life was skewed to head in the wrong direction from the moment of conception.

That was how I justified the unscrupulous situations I often found myself in. I thought I was destined for less based on the despicable story of how I was conceived. It was a story my mother should have kept from me as a child, instead of giving me daily reminders of what happened to her every time I disobeyed or disappointed her.

I was the result of my mother being raped by a crooked cop while she was working as a prostitute on the Las Vegas strip. My mother worked the streets to support her binge drinking and drug habit. The local law enforcement was willing to turn a blind eye in exchange for free samples. Occasionally, they took what they wanted without asking.

My mother did not want to have a child, especially under such heinous circumstances, and she never let me forget it. Fortunately, my grandmother found out about the pregnancy early on and insisted that my mother move in with her. She helped my mom kick her bad habits and supported her financially, so she would stop selling her body. My mom stayed clean until I was five months old.

My grandmother set her daughter up with a waitressing job at a nearby diner to help her gain some independence and respectable employment experience, but my mother wasn't ready to handle her sudden freedom. She disappeared after her third shift, and didn't come back until after my first birthday.

When she finally returned, she promised us that she was willing and able to stay clean. She appeared stable, and even had a nice apartment with a separate bedroom for me. Things were good in the beginning, but her constant battle with alcohol, crack cocaine, and prescription drugs never ceased. At some point, she must have given into temptation; she slowly sunk back into her old ways.

Every few years, my mother would try to put her life back together. Sadly, addiction always won. She never made enough money at a legitimate job to afford her daily dose of intoxication and delirium, so she had to rely on sleazy men to feed her habit. They'd start off as boyfriends—but quickly turn into pimps, once they realized what she was willing to do to score her next fix.

It's amazing that I survived my childhood. I spent my youth being tossed between my grandmother's trailer in the desert, my mother's rundown apartment on the strip, and occasionally an overcrowded foster home in the poverty-stricken suburbs of Vegas, whenever family services decided to investigate my home life.

I saw the real Las Vegas at a young age. It was the only home I knew until my world was twisted upside down in a blaze of gunfire. There's something about the sound of a bullet whizzing by you that forces you to run faster and further than you ever imagined possible.

Life is full of surprises!

My life has been as shocking and dramatic as my conception, which is why I never expected to find myself slinging hash in a small-town diner in Canada, either. Surprisingly, my experiences in Canada and ending up in this jail cell were both positive turning points in my life.

I'm honestly grateful for my time in jail. It gave me a chance to rest, regroup, and prepare for the next chapter in my life. I truly needed the break from society after all the chaos and uncertainty that has plagued my life over the last few years; I needed a break from the only life I've ever known.

My dysfunctional childhood led to drug use in my teens, underage drinking, and stripping at an underground club before I was even legally allowed to order a drink at the bar. My mother was usually in the same room, and never tried to stop me. I've witnessed her doing far worse.

Fortunately, I recognized that I was on the same destructive path as my mother when a man tried to take my public dance performance and turn it into a private one-on-one show. He didn't like being rejected, and tried to force himself on me. I kneed him in the crotch, and he punched me in the face. I lost my job for disrespecting a customer and decided it was time to use my dancing skills to secure a safer career.

There is something undeniably glamorous about being a Las Vegas showgirl!

I used my appearance, flexibility, and charm to make the transition from exotic dancer to Vegas showgirl. I was determined to have a better future than my mother, so I kept auditioning and building my resume with small daytime shows, until I landed a full-time showgirl role at Planet Hollywood. My life has never been dull, and it taught me at a young age how to survive and thrive in complete chaos.

Ending up in an Ontario jail cell was the result of surviving and thriving despite catastrophic chaos. The thrilling and tragic adventure that drove me into Canada started in July of 2011. I can clearly recall every decision that landed me in a 7' x 6' cell in that brick and steel encased fortress.

It was a scorching hot day and I was willing to do just about anything to buy a bottle of water. It was three days before my next paycheck; my bank account didn't have enough funds left in it for me to withdraw a $20. Money always went out as quickly as it went into my account.

I was using a fountain in the Mandalay Bay hotel lobby to fill up an old plastic bottle when I saw this incredibly attractive man walk by. He was about six feet tall and had a lean body with muscular arms, olive skin, dark wavy hair, and piercing hazel eyes that I could feel bearing down on me. He looked like he belonged on a magazine cover, yet I was the one who caught his eye.

His interest didn't come as a surprise. I'm not arrogant, but I've always taken exceptional care of my appearance. It was something my mother drilled into my head since I was a little girl. *Pretty girls have easier lives.* One of the more shallow reasons I turned my life around was because I noticed my drinking and drug use was aging me too quickly.

My diet is now mostly healthy choices, and I limit my drinking to only special social occasions. I also exercise five or six days a week to maintain my lean, dancer's legs and strong upper core. I had a weekly salon appointment for my nails, and only used the high-end salon products on my long, strawberry-blonde hair. My wardrobe came from brand name clothing stores inside the poshest hotels on the strip. My obsession with looking irresistible at all times was the main reason I was too broke to buy a bottle of water.

I earned a pretty good wage for a dancer, and hung out with affluent men who appreciated the effort I put into looking my best. I never worried about how I would survive when my funds were running low. My career as a Planet Hollywood showgirl had strengthened my talent for influencing men to willingly part with their money, even when they are not getting anything in return. Once I locked eyes with a man, it was pretty easy to get whatever I wanted.

I actually had many profitable skills, despite my lack of education or proper upbringing. I knew I would be financially better off if I'd take my talents to the next level and give these men what they really wanted, but I knew the horrors that came with that lifestyle. I saw the toll the sex trade had taken on my mother, and didn't want to endure the same.

I used my skills of persuasion to safely get what I wanted without giving up more than I was willing to offer. That was how I lived my life until I met Esteban Ramirez. Esteban was the Spanish stud who was staring at me through the crowds of the busy hotel lobby.

I gave him a soft smile and my best come-on-over glance, before focusing back on my overflowing water bottle. I took a slow sip of water, quickly looked at him one more time, and then started to walk in the opposite direction. I walked slowly, so that my hips would bounce gently from side to side. I didn't need to look behind me to know that he was following me. I stopped at the hotel gift shop and browsed at a few things in the entranceway to give him enough time to catch up. He reached me just as I was walking out of the store.

"Excuse me, but I couldn't let such a stunning woman walk away without a closer look."

"Why, thank you. Flattery is always welcome."

"Would a cool beverage on this hot afternoon also be welcome?"

"I am quite thirsty, and water really isn't cutting it."

"Well, then allow me to get you a more satisfying drink. Would you like to accompany me to Red?"

Red Square is a swanky vodka bar located in Mandalay Bay. It was one of my favorite places, and the reason I wandered down to this end of the strip. Red Square was a great place to search for tall, dark strangers with more money than common sense. My fridge was practically empty and I needed to find someone willing to feed a poor, helpless Vegas showgirl. It was all an act—and it worked like a charm, time and time again. It was about to work again.

"That sounds perfect, except I headed out for a short walk along the strip, got lost in thought, and ended up miles from home without my purse."

"It's my treat, of course."

"You're so kind. I never feel safe walking alone with money, which is a smart practice until I desperately need something to quench my thirst and don't have enough money for a bottle of water. I'm not usually a fan of water from a fountain, but my lips were so dry."

As I mention that my lips were dry, I slowly ran my tongue along my upper lip. I watched as his eyes followed my tongue's path.

"It's my pleasure. My name is Esteban."

"Thank you, Esteban. My name is Samantha, although you can call me Sam."

We walked and talked on our way to the bar. He was very charming and had a slight Spanish accent. Each word rolled off his tongue in a seductive way that drew you in closer to him. I could tell instantly that I would enjoy an evening in his company.

I ordered a vodka-water with a twist of lime. Esteban ordered a dry vodka martini.

"So Sam, what are you plans for the remainder of the day?"

"I haven't thought that far in advance. It's my day off, so I slept in, did some laundry, and then went for a walk. The rest of the day is open for anything. What are your plans?"

"Nothing that would be as enjoyable as sitting here with you."

The witty banter and suggestive innuendos continued into our second round of drinks. He was a real estate developer and philanthropist. He'd never married, and had no children. Most of the men I met in Las Vegas were divorced, with a wide array of excess baggage that usually drove a wedge between us quickly. It was nice to meet another unattached soul. I was almost thirty, and fairly certain children wouldn't be a part of my future.

"It's still the middle of the afternoon, so we have plenty of time to enjoy the best of Vegas. Let's think of something fun to do off the strip. I just need to swing by my place to grab some money.

I don't want you footing the bill for our entire night," I offered, feeling confident he'd decline my insincere gesture.

"Seriously, Sam, it's my pleasure. I don't worry about money when I'm planning to have a good time. What did you have in mind?"

"I wish I didn't have to worry about money. I've always wanted to go on the Desert Princess Cruise Boat in Boulder City. Would that interest you?"

"I actually have my own little boat. It's docked at Callville Bay Marina. Wouldn't that be an even better way for us to make the most of our day?"

Wow! He was a witty, attractive, unattached man who had an impressive job and his own boat. Esteban was looking very promising; he might be worth more than my usual wine-dine-and-dash routine. Normally, I would make an excuse to leave once I was satisfied and ready to call it a day. Sometimes I would end up sneaking away, if I thought the guy might be forceful or aggressive. I only slept with men who earned a second date, and very few did.

"That sounds absolutely amazing!"

Fortunately, I'd picked the perfect outfit for boating despite having no agenda to do so. It was never easy to choose clothes for my "sugar daddy finding" missions, since I never knew where I would end up. I tried to pick clothes that were comfortable, stylish, and versatile. Today I was wearing navy blue Neon Buddha capris with a white Eileen Fisher halter top and a flat pair of strappy Fendi sandals. I was a little nervous about going out on a stranger's boat, but felt my outfit screamed, "*this must be fate!*"

Esteban's driver was waiting in front of the hotel with an armed guard who opened the back door of his black Lexus for us. The guard got in on the passenger side while we slid in the back. I didn't know too many real estate professionals who needed a bodyguard, but I was already sensing there was something different about Esteban. Everything about him seemed extravagant.

This was the first time in years that I disregarded the countless risks and allowed myself to be stranded alone with a man I didn't know. I usually insisted that we stay in public places, where I had a pre-planned escape route. There was something about Esteban that made me instantly trust him. He carried himself with dignity and sophistication. The thought of being alone with him on a little boat didn't scare me the way that it should have. In fact, it made me tingly with anticipation.

In reality, Esteban's "little boat" was an 80-foot yacht. It wasn't my first time on a fancy boat, or the first time an attractive man had swept me off to somewhere exotic, but it felt significantly more exciting. I was genuinely grinning from ear to ear as he held my hand, helping me step onto his boat.

"Welcome aboard the Carlotta, sweet Sam."

His smile seemed even bigger than mine.

"Thank you. What an impressive yacht you have here, and I love her name. What's the significance?"

"It's my mother's name."

"Aw, that is so sweet."

"She did a pretty great job raising me. She pushed me hard, and gave me the motivation I needed to succeed. My mom is the reason I can afford this impressive yacht."

I couldn't really say the same about my own mother, although she did teach me a lot about manipulating people to your advantage. Seeing the consequences of her mistakes motivated me to want better for myself, and gave me several of the skills I was now using to make a living. My mother deserves some credit for my life, although most people probably wouldn't see it that way.

"From what I can tell, your mother did a fine job raising you." I said slowly, as I leaned in closer.

We were only inches apart, and our eyes locked. He wrapped his arm around my waist, pulled me in closely, and passionately kissed me. I pressed my body into his and let our long kiss trickle down into several smaller kisses.

"Would you like me to make you a vodka-water with lime? Maybe a glass of wine, or perhaps something else? I keep the bar well-stocked, since I mostly use the boat for entertaining."

"A glass of red would be lovely." I answered, while internally deciding I would only allow myself one glass of wine. Esteban had money, manners, and good looks, but that didn't mean he was harmless. I knew better than to get drunk when alone with strange men.

Esteban poured us both a glass of 2006 Bryant Family Vineyard Cabernet Sauvignon. I studied high-end wines in my spare time, so I would sound more affluent and refined while mingling with wealthy men and their friends. I personally had never tasted anything from the exclusive Bryant Family Vineyard, but I knew it was a sought-after label.

I took a delicate sip, allowed it to trickle down my throat, and then grinned at Esteban.

"Mmm. Now I know why there's a waiting list each year for the latest vintage."

"It took me a few years, but I'm on that waiting list for a case. It's too smooth and satisfying to resist. Just like you."

"No, no, Esteban. I think *you're* the one who's smooth."

I pressed my body up against his and slowly kissed him from the nape of his neck to the tip of his upper lip. His lips were soft and warm. I lingered on his lips for about ten seconds before slowly pulling away.

"Would you like a tour of the boat before we explore the bay?"

"That sounds perfect. It looks like there is a lot to explore right here on your yacht. This is the largest boat I've ever been on. Well, besides a Caribbean cruise ship that I went on a few years ago."

Esteban's yacht had more amenities than my apartment. I was currently sharing a two-bedroom apartment that was about a 30-minute walk from Planet Hollywood. It wasn't the worst place I've lived, but it wasn't a place that I would invite someone like Esteban. It's tiny, cramped, and poorly decorated with outdated appliances and furniture.

His yacht was the exact opposite. The cabin had a kitchenette with Corian countertops, a propane stove, microwave, fridge, freezer, and a cherry hardwood drop-down table for two. There was a fully stocked bar, white leather sofa, big-screen television, and stereo in the living quarters. There was also a queen size bed behind a teak bi-fold partition.

Esteban gave me a quick tour, then invited me to sit down next to him on the sofa. I knew if I sat down beside him, I would soon be lying next to him—or possibly on top of him—before I even got my tour of the bay. Although I was impressed by his appearance, charm, and wealthy lifestyle, I wasn't ready to let him have his way with me.

I gave him an adorable pout and slowly shook my head back and forth. He stood back up, leaned into me, and grasped the tip of earlobe with his lips. Esteban stepped back, looked me directly in the eye, and asked again.

"Are you sure, I cannot convince you to join me on the sofa?"

He put his hand on my shoulder than dragged it delicately down my arm as he sat back down in front of me. It felt like he was gently pulling me towards his lap. I could tell that he was not used to being denied his requests. What Esteban didn't realize was how immune I'd become to such advances, since countless similar requests had been made since the time I was a teenager.

"I thought we were going to head out on the water. The weather is too beautiful to waste it down below."

"Sure, of course. I just could not resist the opportunity to get closer to you. You're quite stunning, Samantha."

"I never blame a man for trying, as long as he respects my wishes."

"I will grant your wishes until you're ready to grant mine. Something tells me that you're worth the wait."

"I can guarantee you that's true."

I turned around, scooped up my wine glass from the kitchen counter, and headed back up the ladder. Esteban followed.

Seduction is a relentless game of power.

There has to be a reward for every rejection to fuel the desire. To keep Esteban's fire burning, I stopped at the top of the ladder. I waited until he was directly behind me and then leaned back into his body. I could tell that I was arousing his interest as I rubbed my firm buttocks down from his chest to his thighs. I dipped my head backward, offered him my neck, and then stepped forward onto the deck the moment his lips caused my knees to buckle.

I had to maintain my power.

Esteban slid his hands along my waist and hips as I escaped onto the deck and exclaimed, "I can't wait for us to set sail!"

Esteban and I spent the afternoon exploring Las Vegas Bay and Lake Mead. Even though it wasn't my first tour of the impressive landscape and massive mountain, it felt like I was seeing it for the first time. I was amazed at how Esteban knew so many details about the history and geography of the area. The tours that I usually took were party boats, with alcohol and loud music. Listening to Esteban describe each nook of the bay was much more entertaining.

He was in the middle of telling me that the remains of St. Thomas, Nevada could still be seen when the water level of Lake Mead dropped too low; I was completely engrossed in the story when his cellphone went off. It wasn't the first time it had rung since we left the marina. Esteban had just glanced at the phone the previous times and slipped it back in his jacket. This time, he excused himself to take the call.

"¿Qué necesitas?"

There was a long pause before I heard him say, "Manejarlo, estaré allí en una hora."

Esteban looked intense and angry while he was on the phone, but he instantly returned to his charming self once he put the phone back in his pocket.

"I'm sorry, sweet Sam, but I must cut our grand adventure short. There is a pressing business matter I must resolve."

"Of course, I understand. Although I must admit I'm sad to see it come to such a sudden end."

"Let's attempt this again tomorrow. I have a few morning meetings, but I should be free by 1:00 pm. Do you work tomorrow?"

"I'm performing the next six evenings, but I don't have to be there until 4:00 pm. We could grab lunch together?"

"Excellent. Have you been to Marché Bacchus?"

"It's one of my favorite places to eat, but I don't get to go there very often. I usually stick to restaurants that are in walking distance."

"You do not drive, Sam?"

"I *can* drive, and still have my license, but I haven't owned a car in years. I don't see the need for one in Vegas. Plus, I prefer to walk. It keeps me in shape."

"If walking is responsible for your phenomenal body, I encourage you to continue walking. I will walk with you," Esteban said, with a sexy wink.

We exchanged playful banter on the boat ride back to the dock, but I could sense his mood was not as carefree after he took that phone call. I could only speak a few words in Spanish, and I had no idea who had called and what Esteban said to them. Our relationship was only a day old; I didn't have the right to inquire about his conversation.

Esteban's driver and guard were waiting at the dock for us. I got the impression they'd been patiently standing there waiting for his return the entire time we were on the boat. We had been on the water for almost two hours, and neither gentleman looked as if they had moved a muscle.

I gave his driver the address to my apartment before hopping back into his Lexus. Esteban's hand rested on my knee as he gazed out the window. He looked lost in thought, so I did some thinking of my own. I didn't know what Esteban was thinking about, but I was reflecting on the man I just met. I had found a wealthy, charming, handsome man who treated me like a lady, and was wondering if I could make this relationship work long-term. He gave me a long, sensual kiss after he walked me to my front door, and we made plans for him to pick me up the following day at 1 pm.

I felt as giddy as a schoolgirl while I watched him walk back to his car through the front window. I was still hungry, but I had no desire to go back to the strip to look for another sugar daddy. I ate an overripe banana and two slices of buttered toast before retiring to my room. It wasn't the glamorous dinner that I was hoping to score, but I had a feeling I'd eat for a long time if I stuck with Esteban.

MY SPANISH STUD

Esteban and his driver picked me up the following day at exactly 1 pm. I asked if everything had gone okay with his business emergency, and he simply nodded yes. He quickly changed the conversation by complimenting my simple yet sexy sundress.

"I find it hard to resist you in everyday clothing. I can't imagine how sexy you must look as a showgirl."

"You'll have to watch me perform one night."

"I am hoping that I will be able to swing by tonight's performance."

I'm a confident, fairly-seasoned performer, but I felt an instant knot form in my stomach at the thought of Esteban being in the audience. There was something different about him. He had class and sophistication far beyond that of the men I usually attracted. He also treated me with respect.

I wasn't sure he would demonstrate the same respect for me if he saw me shaking my assets in an outfit designed to expose as much of my body as possible without breaking the law. I was certain it would increase his physical desires; however, it might squash the chances of our relationship being worthy of sex.

I only slept with men whom I was seriously interested in pursuing. I was already exploring the possibilities of this being something more, and I felt Esteban was as well. He didn't strike me as the type to seek out wine-and-dine one night stands. Would he still feel the same way after watching me on stage, or would he assume I was just another flashy, trashy Vegas showgirl?

"Which show tonight?"

"I am not sure when I will be able to make it, but I do intend to stop in to see you in action, if my schedule permits."

"Wonderful," I replied, with a flirtatious half-smile. I wasn't sure how wonderful it would actually be, though.

We arrived at the upscale restaurant on the lake and were seated at a cozy table for two. Our surroundings looked like a scene from a romantic movie. The food was surreal, and the conversation never missed a beat. This brief fleeting moment seemed too magical to be reality. Hours flew by as if they were merely seconds.

Esteban glanced down at his sleek Rolex, followed by an adorably sexy pout. "It's already almost three o'clock. Do you still need to go back to your place before work?" Esteban asked, after checking a missed call on his phone.

"No, I can go straight to the hotel. Everything I need is already in the dressing room."

"Perfect. That means I can spend a little more time enjoying your company."

Esteban scooped up my hand in his and stroked my palm with the tip of his thumb. My face instantly formed a giddy smile as soon as he touched me or look deeply into my eyes. It was only the second time I'd been out with him, yet he already had a hold over me. I was usually much better at ignoring any romantic feelings. I would simply remind myself that most men can act like Prince Charming when they are pursuing a new conquest; it doesn't mean their behavior is sincere, or that it will last.

The drive to Planet Hollywood was the first time we encountered an uncomfortable silence. I was lost in thought, and not even conscious of him being next me. I was worried that I would trip or fall off the stage if I spotted him in the audience. It's hard to pick out a person in the crowd during a performance, and the odds were good that I wouldn't know he was there until it was over. I was more nervous about what he would think of me once he saw me dancing in that overly-revealing costume.

"We are here, my dear. Is everything okay? You have been lost in thought most of the drive."

"Sorry… I was thinking about tonight's performance. We recently made some changes to the routine, and I was stressing over whether or not I remembered them all."

"I am sure you will be fabulous. I cannot wait to see it."

Esteban leaned in for another long passionate kiss that started with my lips and trickled down my neck. His lingering kisses gave me goose bumps.

"Until tonight, sweet Sam" Esteban whispered in my ear.

I gave him a soft peck on cheek, and before I could reach for the car door handle, Esteban's driver opened it for me. He seemed to anticipate our needs. I got out of the car and was surprised to see Esteban's armed bodyguard getting out of the car as well. He walked a few feet behind me, and only stopped once I went inside an employees-only access door.

Between the fear of Esteban watching my performance and the uneasy feeling I got when the bodyguard followed me into Planet Hollywood, both my heart and head were racing. I had only known Esteban for a little more than 24 hours, and he was leaving his bodyguard with me. It didn't make sense.

How could his feelings already be so strong that he would feel the need to protect me?

Fortunately for me, getting ready for a performance was a well-rehearsed routine. I can do it with my eyes closed—which is a good thing, since I had completely zoned out. I was a total wreck right up until the music started. The familiar beat set me on autopilot, and I performed show after show without fail. I hadn't seen any sign of Esteban between performances, and his bodyguard was no longer around. There was a shorter, Spanish man with a pencil-thin mustache standing by the bar who I thought was watching me, but I convinced myself it was just paranoia.

I didn't see Esteban until I went out the front entrance after the curtain call for the last dance of the night. He was standing outside in a sharp charcoal-grey suit, one long-stemmed red rose in his hands.

"Magnificent!"

Esteban called out to me the moment our eyes met. An uninhibited ear-to-ear smile appeared on my face, and I ran straight into his arms. Wrapping his muscular forearms around my hips, he lifted me several inches off the ground. We shared another lengthy kiss that made me tremble with excitement before he gently placed me back on my feet. An outsider would have interpreted our overly-enthusiastic embrace as one of two longtime lovers who hadn't seen each other in days. I was just thrilled to see that he approved of my dancing.

"I hope you weren't planning on walking home alone at this hour of the night."

"I was, but I do it quite often. I know how to stay safe around here. Don't forget, I was born in the heart of Vegas."

"Nonsense! It is too risky, no matter how fit and feisty you might be. May I have the pleasure of escorting you home?"

"Esteban, you can have the pleasure of escorting me anywhere."

"What about a nightcap at my place?" His eyebrows raised slightly as he invited me over.

"That sounds perfect, as long as you have a little something for me to nibble on. I just burned off a whole lot of energy, and I need to refuel."

Esteban was my meal ticket, and I was starving. I hadn't received my next paycheck and the last thing I ate was our fantastic lunch, which was over ten hours ago.

"We can get you whatever you like, my dear."

I was extremely impressed to discover that Esteban lived in The Ridges Las Vegas. The Ridges is an historic, exclusive neighborhood filled with custom luxury homes. It's a popular location for major celebrities and professional athletes, not real estate professionals.

Esteban had over an acre of property that was surrounded by a 10-foot-high, wrought-iron fence with a guarded gate. There was a long, winding driveway lined with tall trees and thick shrubs. You could not see the massive mansion from the front gate. I looked over at the armed guard, then back at Esteban, and raised one eyebrow.

"What type of real estate are you in, exactly?"

"I specialize in high-end luxury homes and five-star office rental complexes. I've been quite successful at it, and unfortunately, there is a constant risk that comes with wealth. I believe in being diligent and protecting my assets."

"I can certainly understand how you feel. Your home is even more impressive than your massive yacht!"

"It's a nice house." Esteban replied modestly.

"It's more than just nice. It's amazing!"

"So are you." Esteban said, as his sultry eyes scanned me from top to bottom.

Esteban and I didn't make it past the front room before ripping our clothes from each other's bodies like burning rags. Fortunately, both the driver and bodyguard instinctively chose to wait outside. I was so swept up in the moment that it wouldn't have mattered to me if one of them had followed us in. I wanted to feel Esteban inside me, and none of my usual rules applied. There was something different about this man. I couldn't resist the touch of his hands, the thrust of his hips, or the lure of his tongue.

Esteban grabbed my waist and lift me onto him with ease. He held me against his rock-hard body as I rode him like a mechanical bull. This wasn't gentle, it's-our-first-time-together, kind of sex. This was grab-pull-and-bite every inch to continuously increase the intensity. It felt like my body was falling harder and harder onto him with each bounce.

We were free from all inhibitions. We weaved through the house seamlessly, and finished our fervent tryst in the shower. Afterwards, I wrapped myself in one of Esteban's terrycloth robes and rubbed my cheek along the plush collar. Everything between us felt so natural. It felt like home.

"Can you stay the night?"

"Absolutely, as long as we eat something first; I'm famished."

"What would you like?"

"Whatever you have that is easy to make. I'm not fussy."

"Alejandro can cook us almost anything you can imagine, and the fridge and pantry are usually well-stocked. Marcos can also run out to pick up anything that we need. What are you craving?"

"Mmm, there are so many possibilities; it's going to be hard to choose. Maybe something light and sweet, like fresh fruit with whipped cream, or puffy pastry filled with jam?"

"Why not have both, with a glass or two of champagne?"

"That sounds perfect."

"Please, make yourself at home while I let Alejandro know our plans."

Esteban went off into the west wing of the house while I sat on the edge of his bed, wearing only his robe. His room was mainly taupe, with bold splashes of burgundy and gold. It appeared that every detail had been specifically crafted for Esteban by a high-class interior designer. His real estate career must have given him the knowledge or the connections to create a custom look that signified dignity, power, and modern style.

Once he was out of sight, I scanned the room for any personal details that would give me more insight into his life. There was nothing on top of his dresser, and only an alarm clock, TV remote, and lamp on the night stand on the left side of his bed. I quickly peeked into the night stand drawer, but it was completely empty. I also looked inside the dresser drawers, which were filled with neatly folded clothes. He had a chest at the end of his bed that held a comforter and two pillows.

There didn't seem to be any telltale signs of his personal life in his bedroom, so I moved onto the bathroom. His en suite bathroom was larger than my bedroom, yet it only contained the basic fixtures and paraphernalia that men need for their daily grooming. The only information I gathered from my closer inspection was that either Esteban was a meticulous housekeeper, or he employed a stellar cleaning service. The bathroom was spotless.

Esteban walked into the bedroom just as I exited the bathroom. I slipped off the robe, let it drop to the floor, and then walked over to the opposite side of the bed to scoop up my form-fitting sundress. I slowly slid it over my body, and gave Esteban a sultry stare once my head popped out through the top.

"Your home is beautiful. Did you pick the décor yourself?"

"Décor is really not my specialty. I hired a professional. Would you like a tour while we wait for our snack?"

"Sure. I wasn't really paying attention to my surroundings when we first stumbled in." I said with a wink.

Esteban gave me a tour of the massive mansion. Every room was as meticulous and elegant as his bedroom. Every room also felt equally hollow. There was expensive furniture, modern accents, and decadent décor that took up just the right amount of space in each room, yet the rooms felt empty. Every room appeared as if it was staged for a magazine advertisement. There were no noticeable mementos or family photos.

"How long have you lived here?"

"Almost six years."

"It's gorgeous. You have exquisite taste."

"Thank you. I really can't take any credit for it."

Esteban and I finished the tour in his perfectly manicured backyard. Within seconds of walking onto the mahogany and cedar deck, Alejandro appeared with a large tray filled with exotic fruits, delicate pastries, and a dish of hand-whipped cream. Marcos was behind him with a small tray that held two tall champagne glasses.

"Thank you, gentlemen, and good night." Esteban said to his servants, as they laid our evening snack on the wrought-iron patio table. He gave them both a stern nod and they vanished as quickly as they had appeared. Esteban and I enjoyed our snack under the stars in a comfortable, sultry silence. His eyes were intensely focused on each bite I took.

"Watching you slowly seduce each piece of fruit in your mouth is giving me the urge to whisk you back into bed."

"That doesn't sound like an urge you should fight."

Esteban scooped me up in his arms and carried me back to his room. We made passionate love again and I fell asleep in his arms. I didn't even realize where I was until he woke me the next morning to say good-bye. He kissed me on the forehead and whispered in my ear.

"Rest, my dear, and make yourself at home when you get up. I have work that needs my attention, but Marcos will take you home whenever you like. See you soon, I hope."

"Very soon, I hope."

I tried to fall back asleep, but there were too many thoughts running through my head. My ship had finally come in! Esteban was handsome, charming, sweet, and wealthy beyond my wildest imagination. He could give me the life that I've always wanted. After a few minutes of daydreaming about the possibilities, I slipped out of bed and back into my sundress. I was planning on thoroughly exploring Esteban's mansion, but his guard was standing immediately outside the bedroom door, waiting to greet me.

"Good morning."

"Good morning."

"The car is waiting for you."

"Okay, I just need to gather my things."

"Of course, Ma'am. Whenever you are ready."

I grabbed my purse and shoes, then followed the large, emotionless man outside. This time there was a black Escalade parked in the driveway, with a different driver. Esteban's guard opened the door for me and then got into the passenger side. The three of us rode the entire way back to my apartment in silence.

I tried to get a little more sleep in my own bed, but it wasn't as comfortable. I should have lain in Esteban's bed for as long as possible. After an hour of tossing and turning, I got up and made myself breakfast. I was debating whether or not to call Esteban to make plans for that evening when my cellphone rang.

It was him.

"Hello?"

"Hello, my dear. I heard you were already home. I expected you to sleep longer, after the late night we shared."

"I did, too."

"Was the bed uncomfortable?"

"No, it was actually so comfortable that it has probably ruined all other beds for me. I just felt it was better to go back to my own place. I didn't want to impose, especially since you had to leave for work."

"There was no rush for you to leave, and I am hoping you will be back soon."

"I'm free after tonight's show."

"Perfect. I will try to get there in time to see your last performance. Last night's performance was pure magic. I would love to watch it again."

This time, I wasn't nervous at the thought of him being in audience. I could tell my skimpy outfit and seductive dance moves had impressed and enticed him. The thought of him getting aroused watching me dance was compelling enough that I couldn't stop touching myself. His voice made me melt, and I didn't want him to hang up.

"I'll have to give you a private performance when we get back to your place."

"You know that is all I will be thinking about from now until then."

"Good plan! I'll be thinking of the earth-shattering sex we had last night, and we'll both be ready to explode before we get inside the house."

His response was a manly grunt and growl that I can't quite capture with words. I will say that his rough, primal sound made me reach my orgasm. This was the first time a man's voice had the ability to achieve such glorious satisfaction.

After Esteban and I finally said our good-byes, I soothed my body to sleep. I took a two-hour nap and woke up feeling invincible. I practically skipped the entire way to Planet Hollywood.

I was so blinded by my new-found happiness that I didn't notice I was being followed. It was the same short, Spanish man with the thin mustache I had seen the day before at Planet Hollywood. He was walking about ten feet behind me, and stopped just outside the entrance to the hotel. I had seen him in a reflection when I first started down the Vegas strip, but I didn't get a good look at him until I stopped at the crosswalk just before Bally's.

I maintained the same enthusiastic pace and tried not to act startled, even though my heart was now racing faster than my feet. I was somewhat relieved that he didn't follow me inside the hotel. Many Las Vegas dancers have smitten fans, several of which have turned into stalkers. I wasn't sure if he was a fan, stalker, or just a creepy coincidence. My gut was convinced that I'd see him again.

Luckily, I knew that I would also see Esteban again. I could tell that he wanted to protect and care for me, and being around him made me feel safe. I could perform with grace and confidence despite the potential stalker, because I felt certain Esteban would be there when the final curtain went up.

That doesn't mean I wasn't relieved to discover that I was right. After the show ended, Esteban was waiting for me outside the dressing room, smiling like a GQ model in his perfectly pressed suit. This time he was holding a square, silver gift box instead of a rose.

"Bravo, Sam! You are an amazing dancer."

Esteban pulled me in for a quick kiss, and then handed me the silver box.

"What's this?"

"You'll have to open it to find out."

I gently undid the gold bow that secured the two thin halves of the box together. There was a beautiful, white cashmere Forzieri pashmina neatly folded inside. I immediately pulled it from the box with excitement and wrapped it around my neck.

"It's absolutely gorgeous, but why did you get me a gift? It isn't my birthday, and you don't owe me anything for last night."

"Oh Sam, I know that I don't owe you anything for last night. I am certain that last night was a special moment for both of us. I just wanted you to have a nice wrap for those nights you do walk home. It gets quite chilly, once the sun goes down."

"You are so sweet, Esteban. How did I get so lucky?"

"Believe me when I say that I am the lucky one."

I kissed him again, and then stepped towards the car. Esteban's bodyguard responded to my slight gesture and opened the door to the Lexus. We slipped inside and drove back to his place in a surreal and comfortable silence. I rested my head on his chest while I curled up inside his muscular arm. I felt safe and secure.

Too Good to Be True

One of the lessons I've learned throughout my life is that nothing is ever quite as it seems. I thought I had a normal childhood until I was in grade six (one of the few years that I attended public school), and I made a new friend named Amanda. Amanda had happily married parents in a clean, drug-free home just outside of the Vegas strip. They ate dinner together, talked about their day, and celebrated each other's accomplishments. Their home made me feel safe and secure. It also made me realize that my home life was not normal.

The more rebellious I became as I got older, the less Amanda's parents wanted me around. We got caught stealing and smoking pot together, which was something her law-abiding parents disapproved of greatly. They rightfully felt I was a bad influence on her, and I was no longer welcome in my safe and secure new world.

Reality sunk in, and I went downhill with it.

A lot has changed since I was a troubled pre-teen, but my inability to trust people and places has not. I knew that my safe spot in Esteban's arms was only as stable as all other relationships. One false move and this fairy-tale experience could turn into another tough life lesson.

We arrived at Esteban's home without incident, and entered his house with the same sexual intensity we had during our prior escapade. Esteban tossed me on his bed and kissed me from my neck down to my thighs. He made my body shake with anticipation. We spent the next twenty minutes ravishing each other's bodies without any hesitation. We followed quenching our sexual appetite with another sweet late night snack, and then fell asleep entwined together.

Once again, Esteban kissed me goodbye and snuck out before the sun came up. This time I decided to enjoy the plush mattress and high-quality bedding. I fell back asleep and didn't wake up until just after 10:00 am, when I heard arguing coming from the kitchen. I couldn't make out what they were saying, because every word was in Spanish. However, I could tell by the tone of their voices that there was a lot of anger fueling the conversation.

I quickly threw my clothes on and headed towards the source of the boisterous debate. I stopped a few feet short of the entranceway to the open-concept kitchen and dining area, but I didn't recognize the voices. I took a deep breath and walked the last few steps to the entranceway.

Esteban's bodyguard was screaming in Spanish at two younger men. His gun was drawn and pointed at the temple of the man closest to him. He saw me come around the corner, immediately dropped the gun, stopped yelling, and shot both young men a threatening glare that made them turn pale and scatter. They quickly disappeared out Esteban's back-patio door.

"My sincerest apologies, Ms. Samantha. I did not intend to wake you."

"Is everything okay?"

"Yes. Are you ready to go home?"

"Yes, thank you."

I quickly gathered my belongings and left Esteban's house with his driver and the gun-happy bodyguard. I didn't know the reason behind the intimidating scolding and possible death threat, but I was certain his bodyguard was not someone you wanted to have on your bad side. I figured that was probably the reason Esteban hired him in the first place, so I didn't mention the incident when I spoke with Esteban after I was dropped off at my apartment. Esteban invited me out for lunch before my shift again, which I gladly accepted.

I took a long shower, changed my clothes, and waited for my date to arrive. As per usual, Esteban was on time and dressed impeccably. He complimented my outfit, kissed me on the cheek, and commented on how he couldn't stop thinking about me.

"You've been on my mind too, Esteban. I wish we didn't work opposite shifts. It limits our time together."

"Sadly, it wouldn't matter. My business consumes most of the day, and continues well into the night. While you're performing, I'm jumping through hoops for demanding clients."

"I would imagine with your wealth and power that you would have assistants jumping through those hoops for you."

"There are a lot of decisions and dealings that can only be done by me. I think it is crucial that business owners are personally invested and involved in their company. I have assistants, but I take pride in running things."

"That's very admirable. I love that you are a hard-working man."

"I love that you are a sexy, Vegas showgirl." He stretched out the s and x in sexy, making my body long for his mouth.

Esteban pulled me close and gave me a kiss that made my knees weak. He was everything I had been searching for in a man; handsome, charming, wealthy, witty, and passionate. I felt like the luckiest woman in the world. Esteban's driver opened the door to the Lexus at the very moment our kiss ended and we headed off to another one of Las Vegas's finest restaurants, Spago.

"Have you ever met Mr. Wolfgang Puck?" Esteban asked, after we placed our lunch orders.

"I was actually introduced to him at a party I attended a few years back. He seemed like a sweet and sincere man. I doubt he would remember, but I sure do."

"Oh, he is a great man, and I am sure he would remember someone as magnificent as you. So how can I impress you with the fact that I know him, if you've already met him?"

"You already impress me in so many other ways."

"May I pick you up after curtain call tonight?"

"Most definitely."

I graceful slipped my foot out of my casual sling-back sandals and started to rub his inner thigh under the table. Esteban's eyes felt like they were piercing through my skin. I rubbed my lips together, and then took a delicate sip of my glass of wine.

"Hopefully, I can survive the anticipation." Esteban gave me his most sultry smile as the words slid out from his lips.

Esteban's sexual banter excited me beyond any other man's mere words. His eager and adoring remarks made me feel like I was irresistible. I melted into putty with his every sentence. We had only known each other for a few days, but I knew that I was falling for him, head over heels.

We discussed our various interests and hobbies, but the conversation always led back to a potential sexual escapade. Our fabulous lunch flew by due to the constant chatter, and it was suddenly time for us to part ways. Since I had just received my paycheck, I eagerly offered to pay for our lunch. My gesture was politely declined. Esteban insisted on paying the bill, and told me that it was unnecessary for me to ever offer again.

"You may think it is old-fashioned, but I think a man should always pick up the tab when he's been rewarded with the companionship of a lovely lady."

I couldn't hide how much his flattery had affected me. My cheeks were bright red, and I was smiling so big my face hurt. I'm a street-smart woman, and I won't allow the men in my life to feel like they have any power over me. I know how crucial it is to maintain your independence and leverage in a relationship. Esteban's charm was beating down my defense system faster than I thought possible. He was more than just a sugar daddy.

"You're spoiling me, Esteban."

"It's my pleasure."

We left the restaurant holding hands, and decided to walk to Planet Hollywood. I saw Esteban's driver move the car to the entrance of Planet Hollywood while we were still crossing the Las Vegas Boulevard. He must have conveyed his plans to the driver earlier, since he didn't give the driver any instructions as we walked past him and the Lexus. Esteban simply nodded in his direction, and then we started walking towards my work. I must confess that I found that type of power irresistibly sexy.

Esteban kissed me goodbye, and we made plans to pick me up when I was done. We had already found a comfortable schedule, and continued like that for the next ten days in a row. Esteban treated me to lunch before work and then escorted me back to his home for another thrilling sex spree after the final curtain call.

On Sundays, I perform in a short matinee, then I'm off work until Tuesday night. Esteban and I made plans to go out for a nice dinner, followed by a starlit trip on the yacht. This man was sweeping me off my feet like a billionaire playboy, yet every moment felt so natural.

Esteban said he would pick me up at 5:00 pm, because we had to make a stop before dinner. He wanted to show me a dress that he'd spotted when he was at the Bellagio earlier in the week. He told me that he instantly thought of me when he saw the mannequin in the window, and he insisted that I try it on.

"I must know what you look like in this dress. I've been visualizing you twirling in it since the moment it caught my eye."

At 5:00 pm, I was waiting, wearing the nicest dress that I owned. It had a black, squared-shoulder top with a flowing, knee-length peach skirt. It was a Marc Jacob that I'd treated myself to over a year ago. Most of my wardrobe was brand name, but I usually paid $150–$200 for my date-night attire. This particular dress cost me almost an entire week's salary; it was the most expensive item in my wardrobe, including the several pairs of designer shoes that I own. My closet was filled with fabulous clothing, but I was dancing with anticipation to see the dress that Esteban couldn't help but picture me in.

It was 5:15 pm, and Esteban still had not arrived. Fifteen minutes would rarely set off alarms with the company that I usually keep; however, Esteban was different. He prided himself on punctuality, and had been consistently, precisely on time. I started to pace in front of the window, worrying about where he could be or what might have happened.

I was debating whether or not to call him. He wasn't that late, and I didn't want to appear needy or neurotic. Fortunately, I was able to resist my paranoid urges until he pulled in the driveway at 5:40 pm. He looked miserable when he got out of the car, and walked up to the door with an intense look on his face. I acted casual when he opened the door, and he responded with what looked like a sincere smile. I could tell he was more upset about his tardiness than I was.

"I am so sorry, Sam. I had a business appointment that ran long, and then I had to take an urgent phone call. It was never my intention to keep you waiting."

"Don't worry about it. I understand."

"Thank you. If I knew how good you looked in that dress, I would have sold my business to the highest bidder and rushed right over here."

An unexpected schoolgirl giggle slipped out, causing me to blush. We both smiled giddily as he pulled me into a hot embrace. His voice, his breath on my neck, and body pushed up against mine was almost too powerful to resist. If my bedroom wasn't in shambles, I would have dragged him to my room and delayed our plans even further.

"It's easy to forgive you when you flatter me so much."

"It is not flattery. I am merely stating the facts. Can I still show you that dress I mentioned, or are you eager to eat?"

"I would love to see it."

We headed to the Bellagio in silence. He seemed somewhat distracted, which I assumed was either due to his meeting or urgent phone call. I didn't mind the lack of conversation. His hand was resting on top of mine, and we simply got lost in our own thoughts in the back of his Lexus. Esteban broke the silence as we pulled up to the hotel.

"I am not an expert in fashion, but I'm certain you are going to be irresistible in this dress."

"I thought I was already irresistible."

He whispered in my ear that he couldn't keep his hands off me, and then started to tell me the story of how he was visiting a client at the hotel and was caught off guard when he saw this soft, sensual dress on display.

"I do not usually notice women's clothing, and I couldn't remember the name of the store, but I couldn't stop picturing you in this dress."

As we turned the corner, I realized that the store he was referring to was Prada. I've looked around in it many times, but I was never even bold enough to inquire on the price of anything except accessories. I was too afraid that I would rationalize purchasing a thousand-dollar dress and end up not eating for a month. I knew Prada was miles outside of my price range.

The dress was a summery, three-quarter-length, spaghetti-strap one in a soft cream and pale pink pattern. It was very feminine, and probably cost more than twice the price of the dress I was currently wearing. I could see why it grabbed Esteban's attention; the dress was ladylike, yet exceptionally sexy.

"What do you think of the dress?"

"It's absolutely beautiful!"

"I can't wait to see you in it!"

We scurried into the shop and asked the clerk if I could try it on. The clerk told us that it was a Prada original and only came in the size that the mannequin was wearing. She also stressed that it was priced accordingly. Esteban response was polite yet commanded her respect.

"My dear, this sweet lady's body is even more fit than your mannequin and I can not put a price tag on her happiness. Please bring us the dress."

"Oh of course, I didn't mean to imply otherwise. Please have a seat in our parlor. I'll bring it to you as quickly as possible."

The clerk went to get a step stool to remove the dress from the store window while Esteban and I walked over to their dressing room. He noticed that I stopped to look at several of the items on display as we passed by them.

"Is there anything else you would like to try on while we are here?"

"Oh no, this store is not in my price range. I'm not sure you realize just how expensive it is to purchase a Prada original. I won't be offended if you change your mind."

"I am more offended that you think I would take back my offer. I want to see you in that dress, and the cost is irrelevant. I will, however, make one rule; you are only allowed to wear it in my company."

Esteban usual charming smile didn't accompany his comment. His face looked serious and somewhat stern, even a little controlling. I didn't want to offend him and I had no intention of wearing it around anybody else, so I simply kissed him on the cheek and whispered in his ear, "I would love for you and only you to see me in that dress."

Esteban's sexy smile reappeared at the same time as the clerk. She handed me the dress, which had significantly more delicate details then I had originally noticed. It had tiny sequins along the straps, dainty clasps, detailed stitching, and a tight-fitting bodice. It took me awhile to safely put it on in the dressing room.

Esteban's reaction was undeniable approval. His eyebrows shot up as his eyes scanned my body from top to bottom.

"Wow. You look even better than I imagined."

"I feel like royalty in it."

"No Sam, you are far too sexy to be royalty."

I blushed and then went back in the changing room. I couldn't wear the dress that evening since it was meant for Esteban's eyes only, so I had to put my Marc Jacob back on. I used to feel like a movie star in it, but that Prada original spoiled me for all other dresses.

Esteban was also spoiling me for all other men. We barely knew each other, and he was effortlessly whisking me off into a fantasy world filled with my greatest desires. He was so charming and witty that the entire relationship seemed surreal. It felt like we had always been together.

Esteban purchased the dress and didn't even blink at the price tag. He asked for it to be wrapped and delivered to his house. I was so lost in the excitement that it didn't even strike me as odd that he would give the clerk his address instead of mine.

Did it even matter?

I was spending every free moment I had with Esteban and waking up in his bed. The dress was to be worn only in front of him, so it should be kept at his place. It also made me feel more confident that Esteban was falling as quickly for me as I was for him.

Esteban suggested stopping at Olives for a quick dinner after we left Prada, since it was also inside the Bellagio and we were both quite anxious to eat. We split a couple of seafood platters and Greek appetizers while discussing our favorite ethnic cuisines. We both loved all Asian cuisines, as well as Indian, Mediterranean, and Mexican. Neither of us usually crave heavy Italian, German, or American fare.

We talked about Vegas and the lifestyle of permanent citizens. We told each other innocent and carefully calculated versions of our upbringings, and how we had arrived at this point in our lives. It was a fantastically fluid conversation and it strengthened my belief that this relationship would be different. Esteban was a worthwhile suitor who saw me as more than just an exotic dancer.

"Are you ready for our evening ride along the lake?"

"Most definitely!"

"There is only one issue I forgot to mention earlier. I have to drop off some paperwork at a home along the lake. It won't take long. It was a last-minute request from one of my most important clients."

"That's not a problem at all."

"Thank you for being so understanding. I know how much we were looking forward to an entire evening together."

"It's okay, Esteban. I do understand."

"We'll get my business out of the way first, so we can enjoy the rest of the night without interruptions."

We left the restaurant around 8:00 pm and headed straight to Callville Bay Marina. We made it onto Esteban's boat just as the sun was sinking out of sight.

"I love the lake at night."

"I know; it's so peaceful and romantic."

Esteban wrapped his arm around my waist and pulled me in for a long, sensual kiss. The way his lips passionately embraced my mouth instantly aroused me. I wanted him right then and there, so I gently guided him into the cabin below. We didn't say a word. Our eyes said it all. Esteban's business was going to have to wait a little while longer. We had our own business to handle first.

I let out a wild squeal of approval just as I was about to climax, and Esteban's immediate response was to put his hand over my mouth. Luckily for him, I could tell his gesture wasn't an attempt at being domineering or forceful. He was merely reminding me that we were still docked at the harbor, and there were countless people within earshot of my boisterous orgasm. I know some women are turned on by role playing violent acts in the bedroom, but I wasn't one of them. There were too many aggressive customers at the strip club that frightened me when I was younger.

I fought the urges to vocalize my enjoyment, and both Esteban and I finished simultaneously in silence. We collapsed into each other's arms and lay motionless for what seemed like only minutes; we actually spent almost an hour lying together before Esteban remembered his pending business.

"Sorry, my dear, but we must get this boat on the water. I did not realize how late it was already, and I should not keep my client waiting."

"Of course, Esteban. I don't want to keep you from your business. I'll make us a drink for the ride while you get this boat on the water."

Esteban quickly got dressed and scurried up the ladder to the main deck. His cellphone rang twice when we were ravishing each other earlier, but he ignored it both times. I could hear it ringing again as Esteban was getting ready to cast off. He finally answered it in Spanish.

He was talking too fast for me to make out any words. I was trying to learn Spanish to impress him and was hoping I'd recognize a word or two. Several of the dancers I perform with speak Spanish, and they were teaching me basic words and phrases so I could surprise Esteban one day. I already knew close to fifty words and a few phrases, including *creo que me estoy enamorando de ti*, which means, *I think I'm falling for you*! We hadn't been together very long, but I was envisioning our entire future together.

Esteban's phone call ended quickly. He began pulling out of the dock, so I finished getting dressed and carried our drinks up onto the deck. I could feel warmth rushing through my body and my mouth forming a goofy smile as I approached him. He was everything I wanted in a man.

"Ready for your drink, Esteban?"

"Oh, thank you Sam."

He reached out for it, but was still about a foot away. He was too distracted steering the boat to notice the distance between us. I walked the glass into his hand and gave him a gentle peck on the cheek. We cruised south along Lake Mead in complete silence. The view was breathtaking, and we were both soaking in the sights. It felt like only a matter of minutes before Esteban turned the boat towards the Temple Bar Marina. There was a large dock just south of the resort's marina, with a impressive yacht docked by itself and a pathway that went up the hill towards a small rustic home.

"My client is meeting me in there. He's a celebrity who does not want to be seen. I need to make sure everything is okay before I bring him the paperwork. Stay down below, and guard this briefcase. I'll be back for it in a few minutes, okay?"

"Sure. Is everything alright?"

"Yes, of course. I just want our interaction to be casual at first, so I'm not coming on too strong. Don't worry, my dear Sam. It will only take a few minutes."

I went back into the cabin as requested, while Esteban secured the boat and went on shore. As soon as I got down the stairs, I turned around to peek out at him walking towards the path. Something about the situation wasn't sitting well with me. He'd said it was his biggest client earlier, and now he made it sound like it was a first introduction.

There were enough lights along the marina and pathways that I could see three muscular men standing around the shore by the base of the path. In my opinion, they looked like professional bodyguards. There was also a fourth guy standing closer to the dock, who looked just like the guy with the mustache who I thought was following me last week.

Esteban was without his bodyguards and appeared hesitant as he passed by the troublesome-looking men. The path was about a mile long and two of the guards started following Esteban once he was about half way up it. The third guy was watching from the bottom of the hill and the fourth was pacing in front of the boats along the marina.

I went up a step, so I could get a better view. My head was barely peering over the edge of the boat, but I felt certain it was the same guy I had seen on my way to work shortly after meeting Esteban. He looked agitated and restless. Fortunately, he didn't appear to notice me.

I watched Esteban knock twice and then enter the home. The two guards waited outside, about 20 feet behind him. I understand that wealthy people feel the need for protection. Growing up in Vegas, I encountered many celebrities of the course of my life. Crazy people constantly throw themselves at them, and bodyguards are a necessity.

Four people covering outside security, probably at least one more guard inside, while on a secluded hill in a mountainside cabin seemed exceptionally extreme to me. My mind was off, wondering why this celebrity went to such drastic measures to keep the meeting hidden, when I heard a loud metallic explosion.

Faster Than a Speeding Bullet

I saw the guard at the bottom of the hill slowly trekking up towards the house at the top. One of the guards from the top of the hill came out the front door and waved down to the other. A second later, I saw the guard at the bottom answer his phone. They were talking to each other using cell phones, since they were too far apart to hear without yelling. I couldn't hear anything they were saying, but that didn't stop me from panicking when I saw the guard at the bottom of the hill heading in my direction.

I felt pretty certain the sound I'd heard was a gunshot. Esteban was outnumbered, so it didn't seem likely that he had done the shooting. My self-preservation kicked in, and I scurried to untie the boat. I didn't want to be seen, so I tossed the rope onto the dock rather than removing it from the post.

I crawled over towards the helm and powered it back up. The moment I started the motor, the guard from the bottom of the hill stopped in his tracks. I had to come into view to steer the yacht away from the shore. Fortunately for me, many men over the years had shown me how to steer and control their boats in an effort to impress me. I'd watched Esteban start and steer his earlier, so I was able to quickly back out of the marina.

I looked in the direction of the hill once I gained some momentum; the bodyguard was bracing himself to shoot at me. I heard the crack of the gun three times, but the bullets didn't come close enough for me to hear their impact. That didn't stop my body from trembling uncontrollably, however.

The man on the dock with the mustache suddenly drew his gun as well and started firing in my direction. He was close enough that I clearly heard each shot being fired, as well as the sound of splintering wood when two of the bullets struck the front of Esteban's yacht. I closed my eyes and felt the feta and onions from my dinner rising in my throat.

I forced myself to swallow my fear. I gripped the wheel tightly to steady myself as I turned the boat towards the open water. My hands were shaking and sweaty, but I thankfully escaped unharmed. Despite the amount of crime I've seen in my lifetime, it was the first time bullets had come so close to striking me.

I looked back one last time to see the guard and man with the mustache turn around and start running up the hill towards four other men, who were just beginning their downward descent. I had a few miles' lead on them already, and it would be several minutes before they even reached their boat. I steered the massive yacht as straight as possible, and headed back towards Callville Marina.

What just happened?

Where was Esteban?

I couldn't focus on what just happened. My mind could only grasp the need to get away as fast as I could safely drive the boat. I was scared to look back, but assumed eventually I would be followed. That meant Esteban's marina was probably not a safe place for me to dock. However, I didn't know how to direct the boat to any other nearby marina. I followed the wide path we took back to where our night began.

I pulled into an open spot along the far side, turned the motor off, and did my best to tie the boat to the nearest post. I'd left the yacht's tie-off rope attached to the dock at the other marina, so I had to use a rope that was attached to a life preserver. I tossed the ring of the life preserver over a pole at the helm of the boat before securing the other end to the post.

I waited on the boat for about five minutes, just staring at the water behind me. I was expecting the other yacht to come whipping around the corner any second. I was paralyzed by shock, and not sure what I should do next.

Once I felt somewhat secure that no one was immediately following me, I went down into the living quarters to gather my belongings. I picked up my phone and purse, then noticed the briefcase sitting on the edge of the counter. I grabbed it too. I was about to get off the boat and run to the nearest police station, when a thought occurred to me.

I had no idea what I was just involved in. I didn't know if Esteban was involved in something illegal. I didn't know who the people were at the dock, or if they had even followed me. I didn't even know if Esteban was alive. I needed answers before I made my next move, especially if it involved the police. Growing up in Las Vegas had taught me that not all police officers had the best intentions, and I couldn't be certain justice would be served.

I decided to call Esteban's cellphone instead. I still didn't know if what I heard was a gunshot—and even if it was, that didn't mean he was the person they shot. I rationalized the situation, picked up the phone, and called my sexy Spanish stud, praying he would answer.

My hopeful spirit was crushed as soon as some strange man answered the phone.

"Who's this?"

"Can I talk to Esteban?"

"No; is this the person who was on the boat?"

"No."

I panicked and hung up the phone. It rang a few seconds later, displaying Esteban's number. I let it go to voicemail. The message the man left sent shivers up my spine. It was stern and straightforward.

"I think you have something of ours. We need you to return it immediately."

It took me a moment to realize he was referring to the briefcase Esteban asked me to guard on the boat. To my surprise and good fortune, it wasn't locked. I popped it open and discovered more cash than I had ever seen in my life: neatly stacked hundred-dollar bills. I quickly calculated that I was holding about $300,000. My heart raced out of control.

I still wasn't sure exactly what was going on, but I felt certain that staying on the boat was a bad idea. I grabbed my things and the case full of cash, bolted up the cabin stairs, and leapt onto the dock. I figured my best bet was to act casual and walk amongst the resort crowd until I figured out a safe place to go for the night.

As I approached the resort, I glanced at Esteban's yacht one last time. An even larger vessel was pulling around the bend, headed straight towards it. It looked just like the yacht I'd seen less than an hour earlier at Temple Bar Marina. I watched from a safe distance as the luxury boat pulled behind Esteban's yacht. Two men grabbed the stern, pulled it towards them, and jumped onto the deck of his yacht.

I was watching from about 50 feet away. I knew it wouldn't take long for them to search the boat. I walked quickly, yet as casually as I could fake, to the front lobby and asked the concierge to request a taxi. One just happened to be pulling up; I was headed towards home before the frightening men finished searching Esteban's boat.

I weighed the odds that the men following me would know where I lived and assumed it was a safe enough place to go, at least for the time being. I gave the taxi driver my address and tried to piece together everything that had happened in the last hour. I was gripping the briefcase so tightly that my knuckles had turned white.

The cab ride was almost an hour long, and it was close to midnight by the time I made it back to my place. I tried to sneak in without waking my roommate, but she was waiting in the kitchen. The air was thick with smoke and she was sucking furiously on a cigarette. Her leg bounced up and down with each inhale.

"What's going on?"

She squished the cigarette aggressively into the ashtray so she could look me directly in the eye. "That's what I need to ask *you*," she said accusingly.

"Huh?"

"Why did three men in business suits show up twenty minutes ago, hold me at gunpoint, and then search the apartment looking for you?"

"Seriously?"

"Yes! And they left a message for you. 'Tell Samantha that we'll be back soon, and she better still have our package.' Sam, they cut the phone lines, smashed the television, and told me they would kill me and everyone I love if I called the police."

"Fuck! That means I can't stay here."

"Yes, and that means *I* can't stay here either!"

Lisa was pacing around the room throwing random knickknacks into a duffle bag. I could see that her hands were trembling; she was struggling to grasp the items she was trying to pack. Suddenly, she stopped her chaotic fit and looked suspiciously at the briefcase.

"What did you do, Sam?"

"I didn't do anything, but I have to get out of here."

"Is it safe for me to stay? What's in the briefcase?"

"Nothing important, but I really don't think we're safe here. You need to find somewhere else, at least for tonight, and I'll get as far away as possible."

"My brother's on his way from Sedona. I called him on my cellphone after those goons left."

I ran to my bedroom and quickly changed into comfortable yoga pants, a tank-top, sweater, and running shoes. I tossed my makeup bag, a few pairs of socks, some underwear, a couple of shirts, a pair of heels, and my favorite jeans into a big drawstring canvas gym bag. I grabbed my passport, a thin jacket, and the little bit of cash I could find around the room.

I wasn't even thinking about the fact that I had $300,000 in cash at my disposal. I had placed the briefcase on my bed when I changed my clothes and almost forgot to take it with me after I finished packing my getaway bag. Once I remembered the case's contents, I held onto it so tightly that my fingernails were digging into my palm. Lisa's brother arrived while I was packing up my things. The two of them were waiting for me just inside the door to our apartment.

"Do you want me to drop you off somewhere? Maybe the train station or airport? I don't want to leave you here. It's not safe."

"I guess the train station. Probably best to get out of the city before figuring out my next move."

"What is your next move? Can you go to the cops?"

"Not sure, but we can brainstorm in the car. Let's get out before they come back."

The three of us scurried into her brother's mini-van and drove away like we'd just robbed the place. All three of us were evaluating every other vehicle on the road to make sure we weren't being followed. We also decided that

Lisa would stay at her brother's until I could make sure our place was safe. Well, that's if I could *ever* ensure our apartment was safe.

We decided it was best to get out of the city completely before stopping, so we drove for almost two hours straight until we reached the train station in Kingman, Arizona. Lisa hugged me goodbye, and asked me to get in touch with her once I found a place to hide out.

"Do you really think it's a good idea for you two to stay in contact?" Lisa's brother interrupted our farewell hug, giving us both a look of disapproval.

"I honestly don't know. It's probably better if we don't talk until we can be certain it's safe." I gave Lisa a quick peck on the cheek and squeezed her hand, then walked away. Something in my gut told me it would be the last time I saw her.

When I walked inside the train station, my first instinct was to ask the clerk for the first train out of town. As I was standing in line, I remembered watching a television show where someone asked for the first flight out of a specific city and was immediately flagged as a potential terrorist. This was after the 9/11 attacks, and I didn't want to draw any extra attention to myself.

I knew the train from Kingman went to Albuquerque, New Mexico because a dancer I worked with took it occasionally to visit her family. A few years back, I went on a road trip with another dancer to drop her off. It was the first city that popped into my head, so I bought a ticket going there. I got extremely lucky; the train departed at 2:30 am, and it was already 2:10 am. I had just enough time to hop on the train before it pulled out of the station.

I let out a huge sigh of relief once I sunk into my seat. I still didn't know for sure if the men at the marina had killed Esteban, although the odds he was still alive were looking pretty slim. Technically, I had just taken off with his yacht and $300,000 of his money, and was now on the run. For all I knew, those men, Esteban, and the police were after me.

It was a nine-hour train ride, but I couldn't sleep, despite being physically and mentally exhausted. I was on high alert, gripping the briefcase tightly with both hands. My cellphone had rung twice, once with Esteban's number and once with another I didn't recognize, since I'd left Las Vegas. I was too scared to answer it, and whoever called didn't leave me a voice message.

I felt relatively safe once the train finally pulled into the Albuquerque station, and let out such a loud sigh of relief that the person next to me laughed. I smiled back. I had never been there before, and there would be no reason for anyone to look for me in New Mexico.

I only had two things on my mind when I stepped off the train: food and sleep. I asked the clerk for directions to the closest restaurant and hotel. She advised me there was an Econo Lodge and a DoubleTree Hilton that were both about a mile away, as well as a diner, deli, and pizzeria within walking distance.

I picked up a turkey sandwich and Diet Coke from the deli and headed towards the DoubleTree. It was about a fifteen-minute walk. The sun felt incredible on my skin, and it felt good to stretch my legs after being cramped on the train for so long. I checked into the hotel, locked the door, devoured my sandwich, and instantly crashed onto the luxurious bed. I didn't even bother to take my bra off. All I wanted was sleep.

NEW DAY, NEW CHALLENGES

It was shortly after noon when I checked in; I slept straight through until 5:30 pm. I took a shower when I first got up, and felt somewhat refreshed and energized. Unfortunately, the feeling didn't last very long. I quickly remembered the events from the night before and how I'd ended up in Albuquerque, New Mexico. I was starting to have serious feelings for Esteban, and now he was possibly dead. I needed answers.

I was too nervous to call his cellphone, so I sent him a hopeful text instead. **Are you there?**

Within a few seconds, I received a text back. **Yes, where are you?**

I was about to answer him honestly and then remembered that it might not be Esteban, so I sent another message instead. **How do I know this is you?**

Who else would it be?

Who were the men yesterday?

Just clients; where are you?

Can you call me, so I know it's your voice?

I held my phone close to my ear expecting it to ring, but it didn't. There was no response for nearly ten minutes, so I sent another text. **Who is this really? Is Esteban dead?**

I paced the hotel room with the phone in one hand and the briefcase in the other. There was no response for almost another ten minutes, then suddenly the phone rang. I foolishly answered it, thinking that it might finally be Esteban.

"Esteban?"

"No Sam, it's not Esteban. It's his client, and I need that case you took back."

"I didn't take a case."

"Don't lie to me. Where are you? If you're willing to meet for an exchange, no one will get hurt. I will find you eventually. If you make me work for it, I'll make sure you regret it."

I didn't know how to respond, so I hung up the phone. I didn't think meeting them would be the best way to ensure no one got hurt. I was starting to wonder if staying in the hotel was even safe. I knew there was technology available that could track people using their cellphones. Although I paid cash, I'd used my real name when I checked in.

I reassured myself that Esteban's murderers were probably still in Las Vegas, and it would take hours for them to get to my hotel. I didn't need to race out of the building until I created a plan for my escape. I wasn't sure where I wanted to go or how to get there. I just knew I wanted to be as far away from Vegas as possible.

I started Googling various destinations on the east coast on my phone while simultaneous searching the TV for any Vegas news stations. A few minutes into my search, I saw Esteban Ramirez's sexy smile on the screen. It was a professional headshot from a real estate advertisement. The caption made me burst out into uncontrollable tears.

"Vegas Multi-Millionaire Found Dead."

I was sobbing too hard to really listen to the reporter until I heard her say, "Ramirez's female companion was seen taking off in his yacht and is now on the run. Police are not certain if she was involved in the fatal shooting, but she is wanted for questioning."

There was a blurred image of my face on the TV, which must have been captured by one of the security cameras at the marina. It wouldn't take long for the police to figure out who Esteban had been out with last night, plus my fellow dancers at Planet Hollywood would eventually report me as missing. My identity wouldn't be a secret for very long.

I now had the killers and the police looking for me. I also knew there was a chance they could be on the same team. I've met many crooked cops, and knew several who were on the local mafia's payroll. I had already decided that going to the police wasn't a safe option. I needed to get as far away from Vegas as possible.

As I was gathering my belongings and trying to erase any evidence that I had been at the hotel, several eerie texts popped up on my phone.

Don't fool yourself into thinking you can hide.
We will find you. We have powerful friends.
It would be wise to arrange a meeting before anyone gets hurt.
It's time to come home, Samantha.
Call now, unless you want to see Esteban again.

The texts were blatantly obvious threats. These men didn't seem too worried about me turning my phone into the cops, which further confirmed my theory they had connections in law enforcement. I had to get moving before they found me.

I didn't want anything more to do with my phone and was paranoid that it could be used to track me, so I dropped it on the floor and stomped it into little pieces. It felt good to let out some aggression after crying so hard. I grabbed an empty garbage pail liner from the hotel room, threw the pieces into it, and tossed it in the public garbage on my way out of the hotel.

I hailed a cab to the nearest Walmart, picked up a cheap pay-as-you-go phone and a duffle bag large enough to hold the briefcase, some snacks, a few magazines, and a few inexpensive articles of clothing. I wandered around aimlessly for a while, trying to think of anything else I might need.

I wasn't sure if it was smart to go back to the train station, so I took another cab to the airport instead. I needed a faster mode of transportation. I was debating between Canada and Mexico; I figured crossing the border wouldn't be an option once the police figured out my identity—if they hadn't already. I need to get out of the country while I still could.

I had been to Mexico a few times, and knew it had many of its own dangers. On the other hand, everything I'd ever heard about Canada sounded peaceful and inviting, even though I personally knew very little about our northern neighbors. I felt confident that a fresh start somewhere colder and kinder would be exactly what I needed to escape the heat.

I didn't occur to me until I was inside the airport that I couldn't board a plane with the briefcase stuffed inside my duffle bag. The airlines ask you to declare any cash you are carrying and my backpack would be scanned before I even got on the plane.

How would I explain $300,000 in hundred-dollar bills?

I grabbed a carrot muffin and coffee at the bakery and sat down for a moment, my leg bouncing up and down rapidly under the table. I didn't think it was safe to take another train—but I couldn't bring the money on a plane, and I needed to get out of the country quickly. My hands were shaking, and I could feel tears welling up in my eyes again. I've never felt so alone or lost in my life, despite my tragic childhood. At least back then I could walk down the Vegas strip and feel a part of the energy and excitement. I had no one, and was quickly losing hope.

The airport was busy, but everyone was quiet. It was a little after 8:00 pm. There were only four other people sitting in the bakery, two separate couples laughing and smiling as they grabbed a bite before their flights. They seemed so carefree and happy. That was the kind of life I wanted, and I was determined to turn this nightmare into my comeback story. I downed my last sip of coffee and burst from the chair with renewed enthusiasm.

I headed straight to the airport's information center and saw there was a shuttle bus service to Santa Fe; that would at least get me out of the city where my cellphone was last used. Plus, it was north of Albuquerque. So, I bought a ticket for the next bus to Santa Fe, which happened to be departing within minutes of purchasing the ticket. Luck appeared to be on my side, since I also scored the last seat on the shuttle.

The bus ride was quiet; everyone seemed lost in their own world. I was racking my brain trying to think of a way to sneak into Canada without being thoroughly searched. I figured once I was out of New Mexico, it would be safe to ride a train again and I could ride it to New York or Michigan.

I was scared, but somehow the thought of traveling to foreign places calmed me down. I was trying to view the entire ordeal as a fresh start. I had no idea what my future would hold, and that was pretty thrilling for a Vegas showgirl who thought she'd be flaunting her body to survive until no one wanted to see it anymore.

Showgirls' careers have an expiration date. Every dancer reaches a point where they can either no longer handle the physical strain of the routines, or natural age progression has hindered their flawless physiques. I probably only had a few good years left as a dancer.

Prior to this insanity, my only options were to find a rich husband willing to support me or a busy restaurant willing to hire me. There are a lot of retired dancers in Vegas, so finding either wasn't easy. I had thought Esteban would be my retirement plan.

Now I'd have to use this briefcase full of cash to create a new plan—far, far away from everything I've ever known. I felt ready for an adventure, and certain that I could create a new, better life once I made it into Canada. This horrible mess was my chance to start over.

I was so lost in my thoughts that I didn't realize we had pulled into the Santa Fe airport and people were now vacating the bus. I gathered my belongings and followed the herd inside. It was almost midnight, so I took a cab to the nearest hotel and checked in for the night. I'm usually pretty frugal due to my lack of funds, so it bothered me to pay for another hotel when I had willingly given one up only a few hours earlier. At least this time I was smart enough to use a fake name and give a cash deposit, rather than my credit card.

Despite how late it was, I still felt wide awake from my afternoon nap in Albuquerque. I turned the television on, searching for any updates about Esteban. I went through every channel available and found nothing. It was too late at night to accomplish anything useful, so I finally crashed around 2:00 am.

I slept peacefully until 8:00 am, when the light started to peek through the hotel curtains. I took a shower, ordered a full breakfast from room service, and scanned the channels one last time. There was nothing on the news about Esteban's murder.

My plan of attack was to find out the train schedule first, and then plan a proper escape route. The hotel had free Wi-Fi in the room, and there was a Best Buy within walking distance, so I decided to take an early morning stroll to buy a compact laptop and a carrying case with a lock on it. I stuffed a handful of hundreds in my wallet, and locked the briefcase inside the room's hotel safe. I didn't think it was smart to leave a briefcase full of cash in a hotel room, but at least the safe allowed you to create your own passcode.

The weather was beautiful, so I stopped for a coffee at a nearby bakery. The hot sun on my skin made me think of Canada and how cold it was supposed to be. It was summertime, but I had heard there were some areas in Canada that had snow all year long. I made a mental note to check out the weather before selecting a city to settle down in.

I hooked up my new computer to the hotel's Wi-Fi when I got back to the room, and was about to start searching for the Santa Fe train schedule when I got distracted. I needed to know exactly what happened to Esteban and where the police were with their investigation. I also knew any escape plan would be pointless if the police had identified me and there was a warrant out for my arrest.

I Googled Esteban's name as soon as the homepage loaded. My jaw dropped open at the number of results that filled the screen. I used to Google guys before going anywhere with them alone, but my street-smarts went out the window when it came to my Spanish savior. I felt complete disappointment in myself for losing all common sense because of a sexy accent and some charming pillow-talk. The online articles were alarming, and a clear sign that I had spent the last two weeks being ravished and lavished by a dangerous criminal.

Esteban Ramirez was known to police as a money-launderer who worked for the Vegas drug cartel. His murder was being pinned on the cartel, although no real justification was given. There was an image of Esteban standing with his bodyguard, the man with the mustache who had been following me, and another one of the men I saw at the dock when Esteban was killed. The photo was taken at a fundraiser a few months prior, and they were all dressed in professional business suits. You would never guess these men were criminals and murders.

I Googled his bodyguard, who turned out to be a former United States Marine, and the guy with the mustache, who was an active detective with the LVPD. I followed a trail of names relating to Esteban and quickly discovered he was linked to high-profile criminals and corrupt politicians. I even found an older photo of him, the chief of police, a Nevada senator, and one of the murders I recognized from the marina.

The next name I googled was my own. To my pleasant surprise, nothing came up that was directly related to me. I wasn't linked to Esteban on any website I could find, and my name was not mentioned in any of the articles about his murder. There was also no mention of the missing briefcase full of cash. There wasn't any indication they were still pursuing the woman seen with him at the marina.

Discovering I wasn't currently wanted by the police was the reassurance I needed to plan my escape to Canada. I took my time and calculated the best route to get there, and how much it would cost for all the fares. I took out $3000 from the briefcase and put it in my purse. I stuck another hundred in my pocket, a thousand in a small pocket inside the laptop case, and left the rest of the money in the briefcase. Then I took the cardboard that was inside the laptop case and placed it on top of the cash.

I searched the hotel room for something to put on top of the cardboard, so you couldn't see the money if it was ever opened. All I could find was a brochure for the hotel, a notepad with the hotel's logo, and the magazines I had picked up earlier. I placed a tiny wad of chewed gum on three corners of the brochure and used it fasten the cardboard to the sides of case. I stacked the magazines and notepad on top of it and squeezed it closed. I placed the briefcase back inside the duffel and stuffed some of my clothing over top of it. The train station didn't search my belongings very thoroughly or even open the briefcase the first time. Hopefully I would get lucky again.

I checked out of the hotel and called a cab to take me to the Lamy train station, about thirty minutes away. It had a direct route to Chicago's Union Station. From Chicago, I could take a transfer to Ann Arbor, Michigan. Once I was in Michigan, the plan was to buy an inexpensive car and drive across the bridge into Canada. I figured I'd finally feel safe enough to stop running once I made it to the other side.

The first part of my plan worked. I purchased a ticket for a roomette (reclining seat that converts into a bed) and boarded the train without their guards searching my belongings. I let out another loud sigh of relief and settled in for a 24-hour train ride.

The train ride itself was uneventful; however, the scene when we arrived at Union Station was chaotic and overwhelming. The train station was insanely crowded, and I was completely ignored when I tried to ask a few strangers for directions to the ticket counter. After twenty minutes of aimless wandering, I finally found someone who worked there that was kind enough to point me in the right direction. Unfortunately, by the time I made it to the counter, it was too late to buy a ticket and the next train wasn't scheduled to depart for another five hours.

Maybe this was my opportunity to tour the great city of Chicago?

The idea of touring the enormous city alone made me a bit nervous. I wanted someone from the area, preferably a handsome man, to show me the sights. Since I'm not very shy—Vegas showgirls don't make any money if they're shy—I decided to ask the first attractive man I saw how I could make the most of my five hours in Beantown.

"Did you seriously just call this Beantown?"

"Yes, isn't that Chicago's nickname?"

"No one calls it Beantown anymore." The man sternly replied while giving me a disapproving look. He then shook his head and scurried away into the crowd.

I was stunned by his response. Most men in Vegas will eagerly chat up any woman who looks their way. Up until this encounter, I always assumed all men would do the same. I decided the first guy must have been a fluke, so I approached a different good-looking gentleman with the same inquiry.

"Excuse me kind sir, but I've got five hours to kill and was wondering how I should spend it."

"Do I look like a tour guide?"

My subtle flirting was met with another rude response and evil glare. I glanced down at my attire and realized I was still wearing my comfy clothes from the train. I hadn't looked in a mirror in hours, and hadn't showered since the hotel in Santa Fe. I darted into the nearest washroom and was horrified by my appearance. My hair was a mess, my makeup was non-existent, and my clothes were noticeably wrinkled.

I pulled out my makeup bag and did my best to freshen up in the train station washroom. I applied extra deodorant and a spritz of perfume to cover up my lack of hygiene. I also brushed my teeth in the public sink, despite several looks of disgust from other women. I definitely looked better than I had a few minutes earlier, so I thought I'd try again. This time I approached a slightly older man who was sitting alone on the bench flipping through a newspaper.

"Sorry to interrupt, but I just discovered I have five hours until my train departs and I've never been to Chicago. Can you recommend any places to visit?"

The man didn't even look up from his newspaper to acknowledge that I was speaking. I was struggling to hold onto my purse, laptop bag, and duffle bag, so I collapsed onto the bench next to him. I started to cry the moment my ass hit the hardwood surface.

If you're expecting the stranger to notice that I was crying, he didn't. I sobbed like a child in the middle of the train station for several minutes and no one noticed. I had to go back to the washroom to reapply my make-up, which was now dripping from my face.

I finally decided to venture outside the station on my own. It was a decision I immediately regretted. All I could see was bustling traffic, steel skyscrapers, and people rushing around like they were late for an important appointment. The streets of Vegas are just as busy, but the pace is much slower. The mood is also livelier. Chicago felt cold and robotic.

I lugged my belongings down the street in front of the station until I saw a friendly looking tavern. It was just after 3 pm on a Wednesday, so the bar wasn't overly crowded; however, there were about a dozen other people drowning their sorrows along the long wooden bar when I walked in. I dragged myself and my mismatched luggage to a stool and ordered a glass of wine. I let out a noticeable sigh when I took the first sip, and it was quiet enough in the bar for a nearby gentleman to hear.

"Long day, pretty lady?"

"Yes, very long."

He gave me a warm smile and nod of acknowledgment then went back to the beer in front of him. I estimated that he was in his late fifties or early sixties. My desire for companionship had dwindled since the train station, so I finished my glass of wine in silence. In fact, everyone at the bar was drinking quietly, the only sounds coming from the baseball game on the TV above the bar.

I decided to order some food, since I hadn't eaten much on the train. The menu was mostly typical greasy pub fare, except for a few signature salads. I was about to order a Cobb salad when I had a sudden change of heart. I wasn't trying to impress any of the guys in the pub with my sensible diet, and I wanted something that would fill me until I arrived in Michigan.

"I'll take another glass of your house white, plus a bacon cheeseburger with a side order of fries, please."

"Absolutely! That's a pretty big order for such a tiny lady."

"I know, and I plan on eating all of it."

I ate almost all of it. There were still a few fries and the tail end of the burger bun on the plate when I finally pushed it away. It was a lot of food for me, but I could tell my body needed something heavier in it, especially since I'd ordered a third glass of wine.

I slowly finished my glass of wine, paid my tab, and retreated to the train station. There was still an hour before my train arrived, but I had lost the desire to tour Chicago. I piled all my worldly belongings on the bench next to me and simply waited for the train to pull in. I must have looked pretty harmless, because once again, they didn't bother to check any of my bags before boarding. I was praying my luck in that regard didn't run out once I reached the Canadian border.

The ride from Chicago to Ann Arbor went by fairly quickly. I didn't bother purchasing a sleeper car ticket, since it was less than a five-hour train ride. I spent most of the time on the train watching what other passengers were doing. It was something I used to do as a kid, when my mom would leave me on a random bench in Vegas while she snuck off down an alley to make a few dollars.

To entertain myself, I pretended that every passenger was escaping something terrible. There was an older woman across from me who I decided was skipping town to avoid being put in a nursing home by her ungrateful children. There was a tired-looking man in a business suit who never put down his phone. I figured he was running away to Canada so he could hide in an igloo that didn't have an internet connection. There was also a creepy younger man covered in scars and tattoos. I wondered if he was running from the law just like me. It was a cruel, judgmental game, but it helped pass the time.

The Ann Arbor Amtrak station was significantly smaller than Union Station in Chicago. It was also very dark outside, and the lack of sleep was catching up with me. I purposely chose not to arrive in Detroit, because I was fearful of being alone in that city this late at night. I thought this would be better. Once I arrived, I didn't feel any more secure just because it was Ann Arbor.

I immediately called a taxi and asked the driver to take me to the nearest, nicest hotel. It was a Days Inn, only a few miles away from the train station. The driver was of Middle-Eastern descent, and seemed just as concerned as I was with my decision to travel alone at night.

"Are you meeting someone, young lady?"

"No, it's just me."

"It is very late and dark outside. You're safe in here, but I wouldn't go outside alone once you get to the hotel."

"I plan on going straight to sleep."

"Make sure to lock your hotel room first. Pretty women shouldn't travel alone."

I thanked him for his advice, but it rubbed me the wrong way. I'm sure it was said out of sincere concern for me; however, I didn't like the assumption that I couldn't take care of myself. I was able to escape murderous criminals on my own. I'd created a smart plan to skip the country with a briefcase full of cash all by myself. Surely I could survive a night alone in an Ann Arbor hotel.

I locked my room and settled in for night. I planned to check out used car ads for my getaway vehicle, but my eyes were too heavy to focus. I crawled into bed instead, and fell asleep within minutes of my head hitting the pillow. I slept peaceful until the sun came up.

I took a hot shower, got dressed, and booted up my new laptop. I need to find a decent, inexpensive vehicle that I could pay cash for, with no questions asked. I checked out Craigslist first, and was overwhelmed by the choices. I knew a fair amount about expensive cars because of the men I dated, but I had no idea which make or model would be best for my unique situation.

I made a list of potential vehicles, contacted the sellers, and made arrangements to check out the cars. I had a few hours to spare before the first appointment, so I ordered pancakes and started Googling Esteban again. It didn't look like any arrests had been made, and there was still no mention of me or the briefcase full of cash. I still had to get a across the border, but at least it appeared my passport would be safe to use.

The cars I was considering ranged between $1,500 and $4,000, so I counted out $5,000 from the briefcase. I tucked $2,000 inside my purse, $2,000 in my socks, and $1,000 in my pocket. I locked the briefcase in the room's safe. I knew better than to keep it all in the same spot, since I'd had my purse stolen twice in Vegas.

I booked each appointment at a nearby fast food restaurant, because I didn't think it was smart to meet somewhere private. Growing up surrounded by crooked cops and career criminals taught me to never meet someone you don't know without witnesses. The first meeting was across the street, at a Bob Evans restaurant. My plan was to arrive fifteen minutes early so that I could scope out the parking lot, but the guy selling the car was already waiting for me.

He had dark, greasy hair and acne scars covering his face. I estimated he was at least fifty years old, although his face looked a lot older than his fit physique. He puffed on a cigarette while he thoroughly checked out my body as I approached the car.

"Are you Mae?"

His voice was hoarse, as if he had smoked a pack a day for the past forty years. Mae is my middle name; I felt more comfortable using it with strangers. My plan was not to leave a lasting impression in case my Vegas troubles caught up with me; however, if I was remembered, I wanted to be remembered as Mae.

"Yes, you must be Ahmed."

"Yep, and this is my Taurus. Low miles, runs great, and if you buy it today, I'll drop the price to two thousand even."

The Craigslist ad was for $2,400. As much as I appreciated the sudden drop in price, something didn't feel right. He seemed rushed and eager, which meant there was either something wrong with the car or it was stolen.

"Can I take it for a test drive?"

"Sure! We can go together."

"Sorry, I don't know you. I don't feel it's wise to get in a car with a stranger."

"Well, I ain't letting you drive the car without me. How can I be sure you won't take off?"

"What if I left you with half the money and my license? That way you can report me if I steal it, which I won't since I need my license to register it."

He looked confused at first, but ended up agreeing once I explained it a second time. I took the $1,000 from my pocket and handed it to Ahmed with my driver's license. He stuffed it in his pocket without noticing my license said Samantha Mae instead of just Mae. He told me he'd wait in the restaurant, and I had fifteen minutes to get back before he'd call the police.

I hadn't driven in almost a year, and didn't get my license until I was almost 25. It took me a while to remember what I was doing, and I felt exceptionally nervous driving around on unfamiliar roads. I decided to only circle the block I was on, and buy it if it made the whole way around without any smoke or scary noises. I wasn't a car expert, so I knew I'd be taking my chances regardless. Surprisingly, the car drove quite well. I was shocked that he was selling it for only $2,000.

I took another $1,000 out of my purse and switched it to my pocket before pulling back into the Bob Evans parking lot. The car was clean and ran smoothly. It would serve my purposes well. Unfortunately, I couldn't find Ahmed once I made my way back to Bob Evans.

I searched the restaurant and surrounding areas for about thirty minutes before giving up. My first thought was I just got a great car for dirt cheap, until I realized I didn't have the ownership papers for it. I also didn't have my license. As I pondered my current situation, it all started to make sense. He was anxious to sell it because it wasn't his to sell.

I went back to the Taurus and looked for the VIN. My fear was immediately confirmed; it had been scratched off. A stolen vehicle and a briefcase full of cash is a bad combination, if you're planning to cross an international border. I left the car in the lot and walked back to the hotel.

On my walk back, panic started to set in. How would I get license plates without a valid driver's license? What if the next guy I met tried to rob or rape me? The plan I mapped out in my head no longer seemed like a good idea.

I locked myself back inside the hotel room, flopped onto the bed and burst into tears. I was now stuck in a strange city on the other side of the country, and had no realistic plan for escape. I felt completely alone and hopeless.

I probably cried, loud, snotty tears for ten or fifteen minutes straight. Giving up has never been an option in my life. There have been plenty of times throughout my life when I wanted to call it quits, but I always managed to keep going. I've stolen food and slept in hotel washrooms to survive. This time I had a briefcase full of cash. There had to be a way to get into Canada without a car.

I sat up, wiped the teary mess from my face and grabbed my laptop. I went to the Detroit-Windsor tunnel website and searched for alternative methods of transportation. There was a tunnel bus with a set schedule into Canada. I leapt from the bed and screamed "Jackpot!" while pumping my fist in the air.

The city on the other side of Detroit was Windsor, and they had a fairly popular casino. I could book a night at the hotel and take the tunnel bus over. The only thing the tunnel bus required was a passport, and I still had mine. I felt a renewed sense of excitement and began jotting down a list of everything I needed to do to make this plan work.

The first thing I did was extend my current hotel stay for another night, so I didn't have to rush through the details. I then booked the following two nights at Caesar's Windsor Hotel. Lastly, I called a cab to the nearest shopping center. I figured my story would be more believable if I had nice luggage and classier attire.

We pulled into a dreary parking lot with a T.J. Maxx and a Home Goods store. I found a lightweight rolling suitcase that would hold my clothing, the laptop case, and the briefcase. I also got a deep, cross-body purse that would hold everything else I had with me.

Choosing clothing was much harder. I was used to buying more high-end fashion, and desperately wished I had access to the impressive wardrobe from my apartment in Vegas. The store had some trendy clothing that looked great on the racks, but it was far too sexy. I wanted something subtle and professional that wouldn't draw any unnecessary attention.

I finally settled on a pair of black dress pants and a soft blue, fitted blouse. I bought plain, comfortable flats and a book to read on the bus. I figured reading would help me stay calm and focused (or I could use the book to hide my facial expressions). I then started working on my cover story, in case they questioned why I was traveling alone to Canada, all the way from Vegas.

Once I got back to the hotel, I packed everything I had into the new suitcase and purse, being careful to spread the money out into several hiding spots. I even cut a slit into the lining of the suitcase so I could tuck a few thousand inside. My life had trained me to think like a fugitive.

I couldn't sleep at all that night. My conscience was catching up to me. I've never been a saint, and this wasn't my first crime, but my stomach was struggling to handle the stress. My head was pounding; I was sweating despite the air conditioning pumping into the room. Before the sun rose, I had vomited twice. I knew I needed to take control of my nerves before getting on the tunnel bus.

It was only six o'clock in the morning, but I couldn't lie in bed any longer. I decided to do a twenty-minute bodyweight workout, since I was already hopping up and down with nervous energy. Working up a sweat usually helped me focus.

Once I was done, I went down to the hotel lobby to get a coffee and a cream cheese bagel. I slowly sipped on the coffee, but barely picked at the bagel. My stomach was a mess. I showered and got dressed, then rehearsed the lies I'd prepared for the customs officers. I paced back in forth in front of the hotel bed, debating whether or not I could really pull this off. Finally, I couldn't delay it any longer. I called the cab and pretended to wait calmly in the lobby for its arrival. My left leg vibrated nervously.

The cab ride took a little less than an hour, which seemed to fly in spite of the lack of conversation. I was too busy going over my plan in my head to focus on pointless chitchat. Before I knew it, I was standing in downtown Detroit, waiting for the tunnel bus to pull up.

There was only one other person waiting for the bus: an older gentleman in well-worn business clothes. He stared at his feet to avoid eye contact. It took about ten minutes for the tunnel bus to arrive. I was expecting the driver to ask me where I was headed, but he just instructed me to pay the toll and find a seat. The bus only had two other passengers, which I thought would make it more challenging at customs. They only had four people to interrogate and search.

I was relieved that the tunnel itself was dark. I didn't want anyone watching me suspiciously. A few minutes later the bus pulled into the inspection station, and we were asked to get off. I rolled my suitcase with me, hoping the sound of the wheels on the tile would distract from the rapid beating of my heart.

"Passport, please."

I handed it to him with a big, confident smile.

"Where are you going in Canada?"

"I'm coming to check out your casino."

"Where are you staying?

"At the casino."

"How long do you plan on staying?"

"Only two nights."

"Any firearms, tobacco, or alcohol to declare?"

"No."

"Okay, enjoy your visit."

The guard didn't go through my belongings, or question me any further. I had created an entire story about how a former waitress from the Planet Hollywood had moved to Canada and was now working as a server at Caesars Windsor. I was going to tell the officers that she was trying to encourage me to do the same. I wanted to check things out the area before I gave it any serious consideration. I didn't need to use any of the lies I'd created, and I was now safely inside Canada.

I could see the casino from where the bus dropped me off, and I felt like skipping all the way to it (I would have, if I'd had no luggage). It seemed pointless to call a cab for such a short distance, so I walked there, beaming with pride the entire way. I was also dripping with sweat from the humidity, but it didn't dampen my mood. I was used to walking on hot days, and grateful that the only heat beating down on me was the sun.

I had successfully fled the country!

I checked in, dropped my luggage just inside the hotel door, and flopped face-first onto the bed. This time, tears of joy rushed down my face. I needed to celebrate this victory! I took a quick shower to freshen up, then changed into a more flattering shirt and the only pair of heels I now owned. I put $300 in my purse before tucking the rest in my drawstring bag and locking it inside the safe. It wasn't prime-time party hour, so the casino was filled with senior citizens. I searched the main floor bar for an attractive man to manipulate, and ended up walking out as quickly as I entered. It wasn't even noon, so there were only three people in the bar; not one was under the age of sixty.

Instead of strolling aimlessly around inside the casino looking for potential men, I felt compelled to go outside and explore my new home. I could see the glistening, dark blue river as soon as I exited, and felt drawn towards it. I crossed the mildly busy street and followed the path to the railing that divided the calm water from the city's shore.

Unlike Vegas, the city was quiet and there were very few people around. I saw a few older men fishing, and a handful of people walked or ran past me along the waterfront path. It felt peaceful. I stared across the body of water into the United States, and felt confident I could reinvent myself as a Canadian.

CANADIAN REFUGEE

My serene bliss was sadly short lived. The longer I stood in silence, the more troubling thoughts entered my mind. I wasn't legally allowed to work in Canada, and eventually I would need to get a job. I would need to find a permanent place to live instead of a hotel. I knew no one, and couldn't reach out to old friends in Vegas for advice or support. I may have escaped the mess I'd gotten myself into, but I was far from being safe and secure.

Within an hour, I was back in the hotel room trying to Google solutions to my new problems. The immigration and work visa process was extensive and lengthy. I searched for affordable rental property in the area, but knew from experience that renting requires either local references or a background check.

Then I made the mistake of Googling myself again. That's when I discovered my absence in Vegas hadn't gone unnoticed. There was a Las Vegas police bulletin stating that I was a missing person, and the police were trying to contact me in connection with the ongoing investigation into Esteban's murder. They had a clearer shot of me from a camera at the marina, and the bulletin said I was the last person seen with him alive.

My heart was racing, my body was shaking, and all I could do was mutter, "Fuck, fuck, fuck."

I didn't feel any better when I clicked on the next link that mentioned my name. It was an article from today's *Las Vegas Review*, titled "Vegas Showgirl Linked to Murdered Millionaire." My stomach rumbled in discontent before the page fully loaded. My name was scattered throughout the article.

Eyewitnesses saw Esteban Ramirez board his boat with Samantha Tilson. My stomach dipped again.

Samantha Tilson was spotted leaving Callville Marina with a suspicious briefcase. Damn.

Police interviewed dancers at Planet Hollywood who worked with Samantha Tilson.

I'd hoped my coworkers wouldn't have much to say.

Police suspect Samantha Tilson is still alive, and possibly dangerous. Seriously?

Possibly dangerous? I couldn't imagine what my former friends said about me to give the police that impression. I got along with almost everyone, and had never acted violent or even angry during rehearsals or performances. I loved being a dancer.

For the umpteenth time in the past week, I burst into tears. I was crying so hard the bed was shaking beneath me. Then it dawned on me: The authorities were looking for Samantha Tilson, the name I'd used to book the room I was crying in. I booked it under my real name, so it would match my passport if I was questioned at the border. I didn't think the Vegas thugs would track me into Canada, so I wasn't worried until now.

I needed to get far away, and fast. I quickly packed up all my belongings, called a cab, and power-walked out of the hotel like a woman on a mission. I asked the driver to drop me off at Windsor's biggest mall, because I was going to do some shopping before I went back to Michigan. I made a point of telling him that, in case he was questioned later by the authorities.

When we pulled into the mall, which was much smaller than I expected, I saw a bus picking up passengers. I figured I couldn't stay at the mall long, since it would be too easy to trace me from the hotel. I walked in the entrance I was dropped off at, stopped at a dollar store for a few snacks and personal supplies (and to get change for the bus), then went immediately back outside towards the bus stop. I wasn't sure where I was headed, but felt certain staying still was not an option.

I walked to the back of the bus, which was fairly full. It was mostly well-dressed teenagers and elderly passengers: very different from the characters you'd find on a Las Vegas city bus. Most people don't own cars in Vegas, and many times walking or cabbing it wasn't feasible, so I've relied on public transportation quite often. I can't remember being on a bus that didn't contain at least one noticeably drunk person.

I had no idea where I was or where I should get off, so I rode for about ten minutes while trying to think of a viable escape. I couldn't think of a way to get a vehicle or a place to stay without using my I.D. The only idea that kept coming into my head was conning assistance out of a man. It's been my go-to solution in tough situations before, so there was no shame in doing it again.

I saw a sign for a pub up ahead and decided it was time to get off. Before I got off the bus, I tucked two American $20s into my pocket, smeared my eyeliner, and then buried my purse inside my suitcase. I took a deep breath, exhaled loudly, and then rolled myself and the suitcase into the quiet restaurant. It was midafternoon, and there were very few patrons.

I quickly scanned the limited selection of men, and chose an older man with salt-and-pepper hair in a respectable business suit. He was sitting alone at the bar, eyes fixated on the baseball game. I grabbed the stool that was two over from him, pulled my suitcase in between the chairs so it was in his sightline, let out a loud sigh and made just enough noise to get his and the bartenders attention.

"Hi, can I get a beer?"

"Sure, what kind?"

"Whatever you recommend. I'm not from Canada, and I don't usually drink beer."

"I'll start with a light beer. I'm guessing you're American?"

"Yes, born and raised in Los Angeles."

I almost said Las Vegas, but caught myself before it fully slipped out. The lonely man two seats over decided to turn away from the TV and join in our conversation.

"Wow, I'm guessing you've run into a few celebrities in your life."

"Yes, I've seen quite a few, but mostly from a distance. I've never bothered to fight the crowds so I could get close enough to talk to anyone worth mentioning."

"Are you a struggling actress?"

"No, just a struggling waitress, hoping for something better."

The bartender placed a Coors Light and a chilled glass in front of me, nodding empathetically.

"What brings you to Canada?"

I pretended to cry, although the tears felt painfully real. I unleashed all the emotions and fears from the past few days in a flood of salty tears.

"I'm sorry, did I say something wrong?"

I shook my head quickly, still avoiding eye contact and unable to communicate. The man slid one stool over, so he could extend a hug to me if needed. His eyes look kind, but something in my gut felt unsure. The bartender asked if I was all right; I reassured both of them that I was, without attempting to explain my outburst. This was all part of my plan. It was a trick I'd pulled in Vegas to get free drinks or dinner.

"I'm fine. It's just been a rough day."

I took a large sip of the surprisingly tasty beer and exhaled loudly.

"I've had plenty of those." The bartender gave me a supportive smile and went back to filling the fridge beneath the bar. I wasn't interested in continuing the conversation with the bartender. I needed to learn more about the well-dressed man who was now only inches away from me.

"Sorry about bursting into tears. I'm a little lost right now, and not sure what to do. My trip to Canada didn't go as planned."

"Lost? Where were you planning on visiting?"

"I'm honestly not sure. My only goal was to get as far away from L.A. as possible. Now I'm in a foreign country, completely alone, and can't even find a place to stay for the night."

"Do you need money? I can drive you to a hotel?"

"I have money, enough at least for a few nights' stay at a good hotel. The problem is I can't use my I.D. to book the room."

"Why not? Are you on the run?"

"Not exactly."

Before sharing the sob story I had previously fabricated, I made a point of choking back more tears and looking utterly miserable. I needed his pity to sell the story. The guy's arm was now resting on the back of my stool, and his entire focus was on me.

"My ex got abusive. He was always controlling, and had a wicked temper, but it got worse within the last few months. He's also a police officer, and has friends in high places. When I tried to leave him, he stuck a gun in my mouth and said that he'd be the one to decide if and when I leave. I waited until he was sleeping, packed up what I could, and ran."

"You don't think he'd track you all the way up here?"

"Yes, he would. I had to use my passport to cross into Canada, so he can figure out pretty easily where I am. He has friends who are customs officers, and part of his job is tracking criminals into Mexico. I'm sure that's where he'll start looking for me, but eventually he'll see my passport was scanned at the Detroit-Windsor border. I need to get farther into Canada, somewhere far away from here."

"Do you have any friends or family in Canada?"

"I don't have any friends or family period! I'm completely alone."

My new gentleman friend was acting concerned and compassionate while listening to my story, but a devious smirk surfaced when I declared that I was alone. I felt a familiar knot of uncertainty in my stomach.

"Well, now you do. My name is Richard, but you can call me Rick."

"Nice to meet you Rick! My name is Pamela, but you can call me Pam."

I've used the name Pam in the past when I was mingling with men that I didn't plan on knowing the following day. I didn't want to use the name Mae again, in case I was being tracked.

"Well Pam, we need to find you a place to stay. I have a large house with a spare bedroom if you're desperate, and it kind of sounds like you are."

"I am desperate, but I don't want to put out a man I just met. Plus, I think it's better if I get out of Windsor. I know he'll come looking for me and it will look really bad if he finds me shacked up with you, innocently or not."

I didn't like the idea of going back to a stranger's house, although I wasn't sure if there would be another option. I was trying to deal with one problem at a time and hadn't exactly determined where I should go. All I knew was that I needed out of Windsor as fast as possible.

"Yeah, I don't want that either. I also have a cottage along the water. It's about an hour's drive out of the city, and very secluded. I could drop you off there until you figure out what to do next."

His plan sounded perfect, yet the knot it my stomach tightened and turned. Why would a man with enough money for a house and a cottage be drinking by himself in the middle of the afternoon on a weekday? Why would he be willing to let a stranger he just met stay in his home? I've always heard Canadians are kind and generous, but this seemed too good to be true.

"You don't even know me. I could never ask that of a stranger."

"So, let's have a drink together and get to know each other better. I can't abandon a damsel in distress."

"You are so sweet!"

His beer was empty and I was almost finished my mine, so he asked the bartender for another round. He seemed charming enough, although it still felt sketchy that he was offering to drive an hour out of his way and lend me his cottage for an undetermined amount of time. I told him I thought it was a very nice thing to do, though.

"Thanks, but I'm sure anyone would do the same. It sounds like it's been a rough journey already."

"Yes, and I still don't know how I'm going to start a new life in Canada without any identification."

"We'll take this one step at a time. I'm sure there are groups that can help you get back on your feet. I know there's at least one women's shelter in Windsor."

"I just don't think it's safe to stay in Windsor. Too close to the border."

"Well, London is about two hours away, and I'm sure they have resources there. We can stay in Leamington tonight, research your options and then I'll drive you out there tomorrow."

The fact that he said "we" can stay in Leamington instead of the earlier plan to just drop me off didn't sink in. I was too impressed by how compassionate he was being.

"What about your job? I can't ask you to spend all that time on me."

"My schedule's flexible, and I can't a leave a beautiful woman stranded and hopeless. I'll make sure you get somewhere safe."

I'm not the type to instantly trust anyone. Falling for Esteban so quickly was clearly a mistake, and one I didn't intend to make again. However, if I judged Rick by his words, he was kind, generous, and deserved the benefit of the doubt. Plus, I didn't really have any other options.

"I hope so. I feel like one wrong move, and he'll find me."

Rick changed the subject to bragging about his warm and welcoming country, how much I'd love his cottage, and what we should pick up for dinner on the way out there. Our exchange started to feel more like a date than two strangers planning an escape.

We finished our drinks, he placed a takeout order for Chinese food on his cellphone, and we enthusiastically hopped into his spotless Ford Explorer as if an evening of fun awaited us. We even stopped at a liquor store to pick up a bottle of wine to go with our dinner. Our conversation was fluid and we were both laughing and smiling by the time we made it his quaint little cottage, tucked inside a forest of tall, encompassing trees.

The location was peaceful, but the property was not well kept. Wildflowers and weeds peeked through the scattered stones of the driveway. The grass was at least a foot high, and the paint on the wood fence that separated his place from the neighbors' was faded and chipping. Once we entered, I saw the inside was quite tidy, almost barren, and looked recently cleaned. The furniture and appliances were modern and in excellent condition. The contrast from the exterior was a bit creepy, but I assumed he either didn't have time for yard work or he appreciated the natural landscape the forest provided.

"It's probably cooler in the backyard. Do you want to eat outside?" Rick asked as he slid open the window above the kitchen sink. It was August and the windows were all closed when we arrived. It felt hotter in his cottage than it did outside.

"Sure, that sounds great to me!"

I fixed myself a plate of food, poured us two glasses of wine, and followed him onto his back deck. The view of the lake through the tall trees was breathtaking. He had a gorgeous patio set and a perfectly stained deck, but the backyard mimicked the unruliness of the front.

I had barely eaten anything all day and ended up scarfing down the three small scoops of beef and mixed vegetables I'd taken in about a minute flat. Rick noticed how quickly I cleaned off my plate.

"Pam, if you're still hungry, there's plenty more inside. Don't be shy."

"I've never been shy, and should have taken more food in the first place. I'm starving, and those Singapore noodles look incredible. I'll be right back."

I popped back inside, took the Styrofoam container out of the fridge and piled three bigger scoops onto the plate. I figured it was a smart idea to fill my belly before I drank too much of the wine we had picked up. Although I felt comfortable and safe, I knew it wouldn't be wise to let my guard down.

When I went back outside, I could see Rick texting rapidly on his cellphone. His jaw was clenched and his lips were pressed so tightly together that they looked non-existent. I slipped silently back into my seat. He didn't look up until he was finished.

"Sorry, I'll turn off my phone. Did you get enough food this time?"

"This mountain of noodles should do the trick."

We ate and drank in silence for about the next fifteen minutes. I could tell his mind was elsewhere, and my thoughts turned back to how I was going to create a new identity and build a life in Canada. So far, Rick only knew me as Pam. I needed a last name and birthdate that would be easy to remember. I thought of using Pam Wilson, but decided it would be too close to Sam Tilson. After great internal debate, I decided I would be Pam Turner, born June 12, 1985. I was actually born January 12, 1984, but figured this was a great opportunity to turn back the clock. I have always looked young for my age!

"Do you want more wine?"

I had been staring off into the lake lost in my thoughts, and hadn't realized that both my plate and glass were empty.

"Sure, I'll help."

I stood up, picked up my plate and glass from the patio table and was about to follow Rick inside, when he suddenly stopped me.

"Let me take those. I'll get us more wine, while you relax. I know it's been a difficult day."

His compassion felt so real that I didn't question his motives until about thirty minutes later. He brought out two glasses of wine filled considerably past the usual curve of the glass, handed me one, and flopped back into his chair. I was so focused on planning my future that I didn't notice the mischievous smile on his face.

"Are the mosquitoes bothering you? We can go back inside if you want." Rick asked as he placed the fuller glass of wine in front of me.

"No, it's too nice out here. I never want to leave this chair."

"I know what you mean. I spend a lot of evenings out here."

"By yourself?"I asked between sips of wine.

"Most of the time, although I've brought a few girlfriends here over the years."

"Have you ever been married?"

"Once, but we got divorced after being married for almost twenty years. I doubt I'll go through that again. What about you?"

"Never married, or anything close to it. I think my longest relationship was only four months. I'm a free spirit and always seem to end up with guys who try to control me. They quickly learn that I can't be controlled."

"Maybe you just haven't met the right man."

I could tell Rick's interest in me was increasing. He had a hungry look on his face that sent nervous chills down my spine. Even though he was attractive for his age and I was enjoying our evening together thus far, something didn't feel right in the pit of my stomach. The sun had almost set, and he hadn't mentioned heading home for the night. I was beginning to wonder if he planned on spending the night there, and if so, was he assuming his chivalry would be rewarded with sex?

I took a full sip of wine while internally debating how I would respond to that request. Although it was a part of my life I was trying to end, it wouldn't be the first time I had sex in exchange for a favor.

"What time are you able to drive me to London tomorrow?"

"We can leave whenever we're ready. I have a feeling you'll have another rough day, so just sleep in as late as you want."

I was starting to feel sleepy, and it was becoming harder to keep my eyes open.

"The craziness of the last few days is taking its toll on me. It will be an early night tonight. Is my suitcase still in the trunk?"

"Yes, I can grab it for you now if you want to change into something more comfortable."

There was a definite smirk on his face and his eyes had wandered down to my slightly exposed cleavage.

"We can wait until we go back inside. We still need to look up places to drop me off tomorrow."

While we were sitting outside, I debated the idea of actually staying at a shelter. Originally I just wanted a ride to a different city—but a shelter could help me get a job, meet other women, and keep me hidden until I knew my next move. I wanted to make sure I could stay there anonymously, and then come up with a way to secure the wads of cash tucked inside my suitcase. I wasn't sure if theft was likely in a Canadian women's shelter, but I couldn't risk losing that money until I figured out how to earn a living as 26-year-old Pam Turner.

"About that...it just occurred to me that the cottage doesn't have internet. I wasn't thinking when I suggested coming here earlier. We'll have to find a spot with free Wi-Fi tomorrow..."

His words started to trail off and I had to shake my head to stay awake. My eyelids suddenly felt like sandbags. I'm used to having late, sleepless nights, but this didn't feel like my body's reaction to a lack of sleep. Something was definitely wrong. I had enough experience with both willing and unwilling drugging to recognize what was happening. Fortunately, I'd only had a few sips of the second glass of wine and have a high tolerance for drugs, due to my past indiscretions.

I blinked several times to indicate to Rick that my eyes were becoming uncontrollably heavy. I then concentrated harder, enough to see Rick's reaction and the bottom of the wine glass. My suspicions were correct. Rick had a disturbingly exaggerated smile on his face and there was something grainy floating at the bottom of my glass.

He's Not My Hero

How could I be so foolish?

I knew better, and usually made a point of closely watching any man who fixes me a drink. I heard him ask me if I was okay, but I didn't respond. I was intentionally holding my eyelids almost fully closed, but peering through my thin lashes, so I could still see him. I needed him to believe that the drugs had taken over without giving in to their intoxicating effects. If it wasn't for my heart beating so fast out of fear, it would have been easy to fall asleep.

Through my blurred eye slits, I watched as Rick put his hand on my knee and waited for my reaction. I didn't move. He then slid it up my thigh. I remained still. I knew I'd only have a split second to overpower and subdue him. He was much bigger than I, and most likely considerably stronger. I had to find a weapon or tool that would give me an advantage. After unsuccessfully scanning the area in my immediate sightline, I intentionally let my head droop to one side, so I could scope out a different section of the backyard.

He had a shovel!

It was leaning up against the house, only about a foot from the backdoor. As I was eyeing the shovel, Rick had moved in closer. His right hand was groping my breast while he rubbed himself with the left, a leer full of sick, depraved lust on his face. I was so disgusted by how he'd played me for a fool that I was looking forward to bashing him over the head with the shovel.

Rick pulled me up from the chair with one hand around my waist and the other on my left wrist. My limp-appearing right arm was free. I awkwardly stumbled along with him towards the backdoor. He had to move me in front of him and let go of my wrist to open the door.

I knew this was my chance. There was no time for an internal debate; I'd only have one shot to catch him off guard. Fortunately, I've taken self-defense courses and kickboxing to enhance my capabilities and strength as a dancer. I knew exactly what I should do, but sincerely shocked myself when I actually did it.

I elbowed him in the ribcage, then spun around and kicked him square in his erect penis. He fell backwards onto the deck and curled himself into the fetal position, muttering and moaning. I then grabbed the shovel and hit him hard enough in the face to knock him flat onto his back.

It looked like he was attempting to get back up. I didn't wait to see if he could stand, I slammed the shovel into his face a second time. His head bounced off the deck, causing thick, burgundy blood to pour out from his nose and mouth. The impact of the shovel against his skull dissipated any effect the drugs were having on me. I was wide awake now.

I wasn't sure if he was dead (nor did I want to ponder the possibility), but he definitely wasn't an immediate threat. I checked his pockets for the keys to the Explorer, which unfortunately weren't there. I went inside and looked for a strong cleaner to erase my DNA from his home. I checked under the sink and discovered a janitorial store's worth of professional cleaning supplies. He had industrial-strength disinfectant, a box of disposable rubber gloves and bleach wipes.

I slipped on the gloves, grabbed the wipes, and started to wipe down everything I had touched. When I was cleaning the patio, I tried to block out the fact that Rick was right there, lifeless and covered in blood. I've been in my share of physical confrontations, but I had never caused serious harm to anyone. I couldn't let it sink in, or I wouldn't have been able to safely escape my current mess.

After frantically erasing my DNA from the cottage, I went on a mad hunt for his keys. I was still wearing the rubber gloves. I checked all the usual places for car keys without any luck, then noticed light seeping out from the bottom of the door at the end of the hallway. The door had a key lock handle, which was unlocked, to my surprise.

The keys were on the floor in the closet, next to a heavy steel lock box that was currently wide open. There were two bags of pills, one with small, pale blue, round tablets and the other with bright pink capsules. There was a small pistol, duct tape, handcuffs, a diamond ring, earrings, and a stack of cash in the box. It also contained two wallets, containing female I.D.'s and credit cards. The wallets belonged to an Allison McFarland and Jessica Jones. Allison was my height and had shoulder-length blonde hair. Jessica was as a blonde as well, but two inches shorter. I put the cash and Allison's wallet in my purse. I left the closest door open, so the police would see Rick's rape kit whenever they found his body.

The thought of his body stopped me in my tracks, but only momentarily. I peeked outside to verify his body was still lifeless. The deck was soaked with blood. Although I couldn't admit it to myself, it didn't look like Rick was going to overcome the repeated blows to the head. I considered hiding him and cleaning up the blood, but figured fleeing and creating distance from this place was a better plan.

I was pretty sure I'd throw up if I got that close to his blood. Besides, I needed to use the cover of night to drive as far away as possible, then ditch the car and take a bus or train somewhere else. I scanned the place one last time to make sure there was no trace of me, jumped in the Explorer, and took off down the rough, country road.

My plan was to drive until the early morning hours, then dump the car somewhere either remote and secluded, or crowded and busy. I didn't know where I was going, but figured the opposite direction from which we came made the most sense. I knew there was water to my right, so I zig-zagged to the left, down long stretches of barren roads. It took over an hour, but eventually I encountered a highway that had signs pointing west to Windsor or east to Toronto. From what I knew, Toronto was a fairly busy city and would likely have big parking garages and public transit systems.

It took me a little while to understand Canadian terminology and adjust to their 100km/hour speed limit. It was eerie how few vehicles were on the road, and even weirder to see so much wide-open space. I opened the windows and turned the radio on full blast to keep myself awake.

It was almost 2:00 am in the morning when I reached Toronto. I felt confident no one was currently looking for his vehicle or me in this massive city. I found a cheap hotel, parked the car in a close by parking garage, and checked in for the night as Allison McFarland. I sweet-talked the clerk into accepting a $100 cash deposit instead of running the credit card, claiming my credit card was maxed out. I didn't want her to try it, in case it had been reported stolen by her family.

Someone would notice Rick missing tomorrow, possibly find his body later in the day; then the search for his car would start. It would take time to find the vehicle and it wouldn't be easy to connect Rick with Samantha Tilson. I avoided hotel cameras just to be safe.

I set the hotel alarm for 7:00 am and passed out from exhaustion within minutes of hitting the bed. I woke up before the alarm at 6:45, sweating and shaking. I'd had a dream that ended with the image of Rick's smashed face. I honestly didn't enjoy hitting him as much as I thought I would. The smell of his blood made my stomach turn.

I couldn't go back to sleep, so I got out of bed, showered, and put on the last clean outfit in my suitcase. I began researching Toronto's transit options. There were so many different routes that I switched focus and looked for my destination instead. During the long, boring drive, I had decided my final destination would be at a shelter in a small or mid-sized city.

I decided that I could take a cab to Union Station, where I could ride the Go train into Burlington. Burlington wasn't directly on the path I had previously been following, so it wouldn't be the obvious choice to anyone trying to predict my behavior. It also has a population of less than 200,000 people, and two different women's shelters. I figured I could spend the day there while I decided where to go next. My only goal for the day was putting distance between myself and the parking garage with the Explorer.

I was feeling exceptionally paranoid, so I didn't bother getting my deposit on the room back. I kept my head down and rolled my suitcase through the lobby as if I was late for an urgent appointment. I changed my plans a second time after I left the hotel. I asked the cab driver to drop me off at the nearest McDonalds, which was less than ten minutes away. I wanted to check out the local news, and knew McDonald's was one of the few places that offered free Wi-Fi. I imagined it would also make it harder for someone to trace my steps.

While I was picking at a blueberry muffin and making sure that Rick's death or disappearance hadn't made the news, another great idea occurred to me. I could walk to Union Station from a block or so away. I called a different cab company and asked the driver to drop me off at a nearby hotel. I had Esteban's drug money to burn, so I bought a ticket to Clarkson, the stop before Burlington. I must admit that I impressed myself with the creative escape route I'd concocted.

The train was jam-packed with business professionals and blue collar workers. Although, I was one of the few dragging a suitcase behind her, I easily blended in amongst the massive crowds of commuters. I avoided eye contact, and no one paid any attention to me. I got off at the Clarkson station and asked a woman who was getting off at the same stop if there was somewhere close by I could buy clothes.

"There's not a lot of great shopping in Clarkson, but Mississauga has a huge shopping center with several clothing stores. There's a City Centre bus that goes there every twenty minutes. It's about an hour ride, and you can catch it right over there. Are you pressed for time?"

"Not really. Do they accept U.S. cash?" I asked.

"Most places do, although they will probably exchange it at par," she replied.

"Thank you for being so helpful," I said.

"No trouble at all. I hope you enjoy your stay in Clarkson."

"Thanks! Same to you!"

It was rare to encounter a stranger in Vegas, especially a woman, who was willing to stop and offer directions. I would always ask hotel concierges, valets, or street performers, because locals couldn't be bothered to help and tourists had no clue.

Becoming Pam Turner

The bus ride to Square One in Mississauga was long and uneventful. It was early afternoon by the time I reached the mall entrance. It was much more modern than the mall I'd briefly visited in Windsor. I checked the store map for a dry cleaner and a few generic clothing stores. I dropped off my dirty clothes at the cleaners, picked up a new outfit at Old Navy, and grabbed some cheap socks and underwear from Walmart. For the first time, I was intentionally choosing ones that didn't look sexy. I used the name Pam Turner at the cleaners. I kept repeating the name to myself, so I could get used to responding to it.

I found a relatively busy restaurant and ordered an Asian chopped salad with chicken. I wanted something healthy, since I didn't know where or when my next meal would be. While waiting for the food to arrive, I pulled my laptop out of the suitcase and did another search of recent news articles. I couldn't find any recent articles that mentioned a missing person or a murder at a Leamington cottage.

Just from skimming through Canadian news, I noticed a noteworthy difference compared to the American articles I was used to reading. Most of the Canadian news was about fun festivals, charity work, new business developments and local heroes. Everything sounded upbeat and encouraging.

I found a few stories about convenience store robberies, but there didn't appear to be much crime to report. When I Googled "murder at Ontario cottage", the only article that came up was from four years ago. Nothing came up when I searched for a murder in Leamington. Murders, violence, and other heinous crimes dominate the news in Las Vegas. It's unusual to find something positive.

I Googled Samantha Tilson as well; fortunately, there were no new articles about me or Esteban. I let out a sigh of relief and tucked the laptop back in my suitcase. I felt pretty certain that no one was hot on my trail, so I ordered a glass of Pinot Grigio to complement my salad.

After I finished my lunch, I picked up my dry cleaning and repacked my suitcase. I moved a little more money into my purse, most of it buried deep inside. I took the same bus back to the Go Train station and bought a ticket for Burlington.

The commuter train wasn't nearly as busy in the middle of the afternoon. I found a seat next to a very attractive man with a warm smile, and crammed my suitcase in front of us.

"Sorry about the suitcase."

"Don't worry, I have enough room. Are you traveling for work or pleasure?"

I gave him a puzzled look while I debated my answer. I was definitely not traveling for work, and I wouldn't consider any parts of my journey thus far to be pleasurable. I must have been debating my answer longer than I realized, because the handsome man sheepishly apologized.

"Sorry, I don't mean to pry."

"Don't be sorry. I didn't know how to answer the question. It's not really work or pleasure. I just need to relocate," I explained.

I considered telling him my fictional sob story (or even the real sob story), so I could use him to advance my escape. It was something I'd done with many men in the past, but I finally realized that I couldn't rely on men to save me. The last two men I had trusted were both despicably deceitful, and had died as a result of their devious behavior.

He gave me a sympathetic smile and turned his focus to the steel and glass metropolis rushing past the window. I used the silence to mentally rehearse my cover story for the shelter. I was still debating whether or not I should lie about being American. I was worried they wouldn't accept me if I wasn't Canadian.

It didn't take long to arrive in Burlington, which looked a lot like Windsor. I was about to call a cab when a flood of emotions overwhelmed me. My legs felt weak, my heart started to race and tears forced their way down my cheeks. I tossed myself and my suitcase onto the nearest bench. I felt too weak to stand.

A week ago, I was a showgirl in Vegas and had just met a wealthy, attractive man who spoiled me with lavish gifts. For the first time in forever, I'd felt like I had a chance at a happy, worry-free life. Suddenly, I was in a foreign country about to check myself into a woman's shelter because the man I was falling for is dead, and I'd probably killed another man for trying to rape me.

How did my life get twisted upside down so quickly?

I had a long history of beating myself up, but I thought I had matured beyond those feelings. I was proud of how I cleaned up my act and landed a spot in a real Vegas show. My life was on a devastatingly downward track, and I'd turned it around. Yet here I was, a fugitive, completely alone in a strange place.

Yes, I cried again. My eyes were scratchy and red from all the crying I had done over the last few days. I didn't even bother to reapply my eyeliner after my last crying fit. When I was a teenager and my life was sinking fast, I didn't bawl my eyes out. This wasn't the first time my life had fallen apart, but it was the most tears I ever remembered shedding.

I pride myself on being a confident survivor. Life dealt me a tough hand, and I played it the best I could. At least, that used to be how I viewed myself. My recent lack of better judgement proved I wasn't as strong as I thought. I had put my faith in men instead of myself. I knew better; the only hero in my life has always been me. Esteban wasn't the answer to my problems. Preying on men's weaknesses in the hope they'll take care of me is a dangerous game; Rick proved that.

I was tired of crying, and knew blaming myself for the mess I was in wouldn't help me get out of it. I may have made mistakes, but I'm still alive. Considering the close calls I experienced, it was amazing I was always able to save my own life.

It was time to create a fresh start, to be a better person and believe in myself. I still felt like the shelter was my best hope, so I called a cab and waited on the bench outside the station. I wiped the tear stains from my cheeks and took a deep breath to compose myself. I was ready.

It was a quick ten-minute ride, which was a good thing considering the cab reeked of rancid body odor and stale cigarettes. When the cab pulled away, I stood at the road for several minutes staring at the shelter, frozen by fear.

Someone inside the house must have noticed me standing out front. I saw two women watching me from a window on the right side of the house, and another opened the front door and stood there, smiling behind the storm door.

My suitcase and I clumsily rolled ourselves up the worn-down sidewalk. I never felt nervous approaching a strange man and sparking up a conversation, but I couldn't even look at her. My gaze followed the sidewalk all the way to the front door. My palms were sweating and I was worried what she would think if I went to shake her hand. She opened the door and welcomed me before I was even within reach of knocking.

"Well, hello! How are you?"

I mumbled "Good," but still couldn't look her in the eye.

"My name is Doris. Would you like to come in and chat for a minute?"

I managed a weak nod and followed her inside, to a large kitchen with a long table.

"Can I get you something to drink or eat?"

I shook my head no.

I wasn't faking the sudden shyness. This wasn't my usual act. I felt intimidated by her kind, gentle nature. I was worried what she would think if she knew all the horrible things I had done throughout my life. The confidence I'd mustered up at the train station melted into feelings of being unworthy of the help I was about to request from this welcoming woman.

"Have a seat and relax, Dear. You're safe here, and we can talk when you're ready."

All I could do was nod and smile. I was afraid I would burst into tears again if I spoke. A few other women of various ages and ethnicities were lingering around the kitchen area. I wasn't ready to tell my version of the last few days to a group audience. My conscience was already kicking me from the inside because I knew my only chance of freedom was to lie to these kind people.

"OK, ladies! Let's give our new guest a few moments to gather her thoughts. Walking through that door isn't easy for anyone."

Doris clapped her hands and everyone scattered throughout the house. She walked over, put her hand on my shoulder, and said, "It will get easier."

"Thank you."

Oh, good! My voice still works. Doris turned away to leave me alone at the long table, and this tiny voice snuck out.

"Don't go."

She stopped in her tracks.

"Please."

I was tired of being alone. My mind had been racing out of control for days. I didn't want to be left alone with my thoughts.

"Of course. We can sit together in silence, if you're not ready to talk."

"I'm ready. I've had enough silence. I've been running for days, and I'm tired."

"May I ask what, or should I say who, you're running from?"

"My boyfriend. He's controlling, dangerous, and most likely following me." I blurted it out so quickly that words blended together.

"Are you worried he will find you here? Does he live in Burlington?" Her eyes widened with sincere concern and compassion. It was an unfamiliar look to me.

"No, I'm from the other side of the border. He might track me into Canada, but I don't think he could figure out that I'm here."

"That's good. We have a lot of security measures in place, as well."

"Does it matter that I'm American?"

"Why would that matter?" Doris looked genuinely puzzled at my question. "We're here to help any woman who needs it. That most certainly includes you."

The painful shyness resurfaced. I stared off into a corner, unable to face dear, sweet Doris. I felt undeserving of her kindness. My mother refused to ask for help from shelters even when she was at her most desperate. I grew up with the same stubbornness. I once slept in an alley, because I thought that was less humiliating than checking into a homeless shelter.

"You're welcome to stay here. We have a couple spots available, although you'll have to share a room."

Once again, I simply nodded. I tried to smile back at her, but it felt awkward. I worried that it may have looked more like a grimace.

"We have a lockbox if you have any valuables, although no one has ever stolen anything from here. The women here are merely looking for a peaceful resting spot after weathering some wicked storms."

I loved her description of the shelter's purpose, as well as the sound of her voice and the conviction in her words. She was a caregiver. Unlike the men I usually conned, she wasn't expecting anything in return.

"Would you like to meet some of the other women?"

"Okay."

It sounded weak, but at least my mouth was forming sounds. Doris went into the living room and invited six other women to join us in the kitchen. Most of them seemed just as shy and uncomfortable as I did.

"On the right is Janice, she's one of our helpers. Then we have Donna, Maya, Suzanne, Katelyn, and Angie staying with us."

The women all smiled or gave a little wave when their name was called. Katelyn looked the youngest, probably early twenties. I guessed Janice, Donna, and Suzanne to be in their forties or fifties. Maya looked about my age, and I figured Angie was in her mid-thirties. I couldn't tell you if my estimates were even remotely accurate, because age was never discussed at the shelter. Most women don't want to admit how old they are—and those who stay in shelters keep most of their personal information closely guarded.

Prior to that moment, I felt foolish that I had gotten into such a mess when I was in my late twenties. I thought I was too old and experienced to keep making poor choices, especially when it came to men. The women standing before me proved that it could happen to anyone, at any age.

I smiled back and finally felt comfortable enough to speak.

"Hi, I'm Pam."

My introduction was greeted with more welcomes and smiles.

"Now that we know each others' names, let me give you a tour of the place and explain what we do here." Doris chirped with gentle enthusiasm.

I nodded and followed Doris and the other women through the four-bedroom house. There were two rooms with two large beds, one room with three small beds, and another room with two small beds and a pull-out couch. There was also a reclining sofa and loveseat in the upstairs living room and a long, comfy sectional in the spacious finished basement. Every room used the maximum space possible for beds.

"If there are more women who need to stay here, we have sleeping bags and a couple cots that we can set up. It's our mission not to turn away any woman in need, and blessedly, so far we've been successful."

My guilt was starting to gnaw at me again.

"Who pays for all of this?" The question slipped from my lips before I had a chance to second-guess my inappropriate prying. I'm portraying a victim of abuse who should be more concerned with whether or not the house is safe, not how it's funded.

"We are partially government funded. There are regular commercial and private donors, and then many of the women we've helped return the favor with donations of both time and money. Most of the furniture and appliances were donated by local stores. We manage."

Doris let out a little sigh and continued her most likely memorized guided tour of the shelter.

"Everyone takes turns cooking and cleaning. Each person is asked to keep their area clean, and has a set time when they can use the washer and dryer. We'll add you to that schedule tomorrow, as well as the chore schedule."

Doris pointed out a bulletin board with the schedules, house rules, and a few business cards for therapists and lawyers.

"When you're ready, Janice will meet with you to discuss what brought you here and how we can help you get back on your feet. She's a trained counselor with lots of experience."

I nodded and smiled at Janice. The tour was over, and I wasn't sure if I was ready to talk again. I didn't feel right lying to these women. I had no problem lying to men, but I could feel Doris' concern and compassion for my wellbeing. I didn't want her sympathy to be built on lies.

"Thank you," was all I could say.

"Maya and I were going to work on the garden, if you want to join us. I think it's a great way to get your mind off things." Angie piped up.

"Sure, but I've never had a garden. I had a cactus once, but it died."

"We have a flower and vegetable garden. We were going to pick some vegetables, pull some weeds, and water everything. It'll be easy." Angie reassured me.

"Okay! I can do that!" I proudly announced louder than anything I had said so far.

"Great! I'll grab you some gloves." Angie responded just as enthusiastically.

Angie and Maya gathered the things we needed, and I followed them into the backyard. Both women were well-dressed and quite beautiful. Angie had a fuller figure, pin-straight brown hair, and soft green eyes. Maya was more exotic looking, exceptionally petite, and had smooth caramel skin, dark curly hair, and sultry brown eyes.

They appeared to be kind and capable women. They were genuinely excited about the garden and all the vegetables they'd grown over the summer. They were knowledgeable and comfortable discussing more than just gardening. I quietly plucked red cherry tomatoes while listening to the two women's friendly banter and debate.

"I have another friend who's moving back to Burlington. She said even though they were making more money, it was too expensive to live in Alberta."

"Almost everyone I know who went there after the auto industry crashed has moved back."

"Her husband found a job in Toronto, and plans on commuting."

"That's a horrible commute."

"Still, it's far better than living in Toronto!"

"Pam, have you been to Toronto?" Maya called over to me.

"I went through there on my way here."

"Could you live a big city like that?"

"I grew up in a much bigger one."

"Where are you from?"

I had planned on saying I was born in San Francisco, but moved to Los Angeles as a teenager. I visited both cities and knew enough about them that felt confident I could pull it off. That was an important part of the cover story I'd rehearsed on the Go train.

"Las Vegas," I heard myself say. The words had snuck out from my lips, and I instantly regretted it.

"Wow! That must be exciting! That's a lot more interesting than overcrowded, chaotic Toronto!" Maya said with sincere enthusiasm.

"I went there once for a trade show. There was so much to see and do!" Angie exclaimed.

"You must have seen all the shows. What's your favorite?"

I decided silence was my best defense until I revised my personal history. I simply shrugged and stared into the tall tomato plants. My favorite show was Cirque du Soleil's *Zumanity*, but true, year-round Vegas residents are not supposed to admit to liking the typical tourist attractions.

That wasn't the debate going on in my head, or the reason I couldn't respond. My brief moment of honesty could link me to my real identity! *Why on earth did I just admit to living in Vegas?*

As friendly and inviting as the shelter was, I suddenly wondered if fleeing it would be necessary, sooner rather than later. I couldn't risk the other women linking me to the woman police were looking for in connection with a murder. There was already the uncanny (and obviously true) coincidence that I ran away from my abusive ex-boyfriend around the same time Samantha Tilson's boyfriend was murdered and she suddenly disappeared. I wasn't sure if these Canadian women followed American news stories.

"Did you get to meet anyone famous?" Maya continued the line of unanswered questions.

I shook my head again. I could use my insecurities of being new and escaping a toxic relationship to avoid their questions for a while. Eventually, I would need a new cover story that conflicted with Samantha Tilson's real-life drama.

"We can talk more about it when you're ready." Angie answered on my behalf. She gave me a gentle pat on the back. "So, what do you think about our garden?"

I was relieved when she changed the subject. She was so accepting of my awkward shyness that my mouth was finally able to form words again.

"The flowers are beautiful, and the vegetables look delicious. You ladies did a lovely job."

"Gardening helps me feel useful again." Angie looked wistfully at the sky, searching for a life she used to live.

"I just like spending time outside. We spend so much time inside, and I love the sun on my skin," replied Maya.

"I love the sun on my skin, too." The tension in my shoulders released, and I let out a noticeable sigh. Well, noticeable to me at least. Both women continued pulling weeds and chatting about tan lines and most memorable vacation destinations. It was a natural, normal conversation, like one you'd overhear at a shopping mall or fancy restaurant.

The circumstances that brought us here didn't define our stay. There was no doubt in my mind that something horrifically dangerous drove these women to the shelter, but that wasn't the impression you'd get if you were eavesdropping on our conversation.

When we finished tending to the garden, we went inside. All three of us joined Doris and Donna in the kitchen. Maya grabbed a strainer and started rinsing the cucumbers, tomatoes, and lettuce we'd picked. Angie collected eight sets of silverware and began setting the table for dinner. I wanted to earn my keep, but wasn't exactly sure what to do. The only woman I had ever cooked with was my grandma; I was very young, and she gave me step-by-step instructions. I was worried I'd get in the way if I tried to force myself into the mix.

I stood there for several minutes, looking for an opportunity to be useful. I didn't know where the plates were kept, or what they were preparing for dinner. I'm sure most women would ask, or at least muster the words, "Can I help with anything?" All I could do was stand there, staring as they whipped up a mouth-watering pork roast, mashed potatoes, roast carrots, and a salad from their very own garden.

I was trying to remember the last time I had enjoyed a home-cooked meal, let alone a dinner this substantial. I occasionally cooked a quality dinner if I knew Lisa and I would both be home, which meant a stir-fry or pasta dish using a jar of premade sauce. The last roast I could remember was four years ago, at my grandma's trailer. It was a special birthday dinner she made just for me.

Lisa and my grandma were the only constants in my life, and the only people who would worry about my absence. Lisa would forget about me over time, but not grandma. She was already 72 years old. My mother was a fleeting burden, appearing once or twice a year, and now I was on the run from the police. I wondered if her heart could withstand the shock.

My grandma was proud of how I turned my life around. She even came to one of my shows at Planet Hollywood. It had been weeks since I'd gone to see her, and now that I was a fugitive she'd probably never see me again.

My body started to shake and tears flooded my cheeks and chin. Maya and Katelyn noticed immediately. We were just about to sit down and start eating; my emotional outburst interrupted their special meal time.

"Are you okay?"

"Oh dear, let it out. We understand."

"Do you want a hug?"

"Can we hug you?"

My lips remained clenched as my head nodded up and down. The pack of women surrounded me. It was the only group hug I could remember ever receiving, and it felt surprisingly soothing. My racing heart slowed down and the tears subsided. By the time it was over, I felt somewhat healed.

"Thank you. So many thank yous," I muttered, overwhelmed.

"Thanks are not necessary. We understand." Doris rubbed my back and pulled out the chair in front of me, inviting me to sit. "Let's enjoy this tasty meal before it gets cold!"

The food was incredible. The meat and potatoes melted in my mouth and nourished my withering frame. The salad was a crisp and refreshing side that clearly showcased the value of Maya and Angie's hard work. Every woman at the table acknowledged each other's role in the feast, and expressed gratitude for being able to enjoy it. I made sure not to withhold my appreciation.

"This was the best thing I've had in months, if not years. Thank you so much for sharing your home and dinner with me. Please, let me at least wash the dishes to show my appreciation."

"You can help with chores tomorrow. I think it might be good for you to spend some time alone with Janice after dinner. Maybe get a few things off your mind?" Doris kindly encouraged.

"Okay." I meekly replied. I finished every crumb of the meal on my plate, then helped gather all the dishes. Katelyn took them from me before I reached the kitchen sink.

"Don't worry, Pam. I've got this. Have a nice chat with Janice. She's super sweet, and very helpful."

"Thank you. I guess I'm as ready as I'll ever be." Suddenly, my mind was racing with scenarios that combined my original plan and the truth, without giving an indication that I could possibly be Samantha Tilson. I excused myself to the washroom before meeting with Janice, so I could come up with a twist to my story that would contradict the image of the Vegas runaway who had been circulating across the American news channels.

I took a deep breath, exited the washroom, and made my way to Janice's tiny office, to the left of the main living room. I went to knock on the open door, but Janice waved me in before I had the chance.

"Come in, Pam. This is a safe place. My goal is to help you get through whatever is going on so you can put your life back together. I can ask questions, or you can just start talking. Whatever is more comfortable for you is fine with me."

"I don't know where to start."

"That's normal. How about I ask a few questions, and we see where we end up?"

"Sure."

"Doris mentioned you were American. How did you find this shelter?"

"I was worried my ex would track me down, so I went to Canada. I realized after I crossed the border that he could track my passport here; he's in law enforcement. I didn't want to check into a hotel, or stay anywhere near where I crossed into Canada. I took a train to Toronto first, then Googled nearby shelters in smaller, lesser known cities. Your shelter came up in the search."

"Did you search using a computer or cellphone that he had access to before you left?"

"No. I bought a laptop after I left him. Why?"

"There are ways people can track someone using cellphones and laptops. Is your ex tech-savvy? Are you still using the same cellphone?"

"No. I bought a cheap prepaid phone the day after I left Vegas. I was a little worried about being tracked, although I don't think he's very tech savvy." I thought, *he's also dead, and it's the goons who killed him and the police that I need to worry about.*

"Unfortunately, it's more common than people realize. I ask every woman who comes in here those questions, and usually insist they dispose of any electronics that could be compromised by their abuser. It's for everyone's safety."

"It's a good rule. I destroyed my cellphone in Arizona. I was excited to cut off any connection with the past."

"Do you want to discuss the incident that made you run all the way into Canada?"

"Not really, but I finally realized that I had been a fool. I fell in love with a dangerous man, sacrificing everything I'd worked so hard to achieve. How could I be so stupid?"

I didn't plan to say that part. It was how I genuinely felt about my current situation.

"You weren't stupid. Don't blame yourself. Countless women, and men, have found themselves in toxic relationships. Love is blind, which brings about both blessings and burdens."

"I need to take ownership of the bad choices I've made. I need to stop making them."

"Taking responsibility is important, just don't beat yourself up over it. Anyone can make a bad decision; wise people learn from it."

I nodded in agreement, determined to learn from this experience. I had no idea where I was headed, but I was no longer the same person. Janice joked about there being much truth in classic clichés, and how her own life has proven so many of them to be true. She could see my mind was elsewhere, and graciously wrapped up our session with some reassuring advice.

"Whatever brought you here is in the past. I'll help you decide on the future you want and how to get there. Do your best to sleep tonight, and we'll chat again tomorrow."

"Thank you." I could feel tears welling up in my tired eyes again. I nodded and got up from the chair, then followed her out the door. Doris was waiting to greet us.

"Everything okay, ladies?"

"I think so." Janice said with a smile.

"Yes, thank you." I whispered in agreement. I was still struggling to shake these paralyzing bouts of shyness.

"Great! I took your suitcase to the room you'll share with Maya and Katelyn. I have a feeling you ladies will get along well."

The moment she said suitcase, I was reminded of the stash of cash tucked inside of it. There was more than a quarter million dollars in my luggage, which I'd left unattended while we were gardening, eating dinner, and during my closed-door talk with Janice.

My heart started to race. Each beat seemed so loud; I feared the other women would hear it. Did Doris search my bag for drugs and stumble across it? Did another woman get nosey and find the money? I didn't want to show any panic or paranoia, so I couldn't race into the room to make sure it was exactly where I left it.

I think Doris continued to talk, but I tuned it out. The entire situation, piled on top of the last week of my life—hell, my life in general—was getting the better of me. The perfect dinner I feasted on less than an hour earlier was being to rise from my gut. I couldn't maintain my dignity any longer.

"Excuse me," I mumbled, and bolted to the washroom. My initial urge to check the suitcase was overruled by an uncontrollable need to vomit. By the grace of God, I made it to the toilet just in time. The best meal I'd eaten in forever was spoiled by overwhelming anxiety and guilt.

The women slowly followed me and witnessed the awful event, since I didn't have a spare second to close the door behind me. I was mortified at the disgusting impression I was making on these incredible women. They gave me a few seconds to clean myself up and flush the toilet, then gave sincere sympathy and support.

"I threw up before I made it up the front steps. I couldn't believe how quickly my life turned upside down." Donna was the first to share. She handed me a washcloth, dampened with warm water.

"I wasn't able to talk the entire first day. Every time I opened my mouth, I burst into snotty tears."

"This is going to be an emotional roller coaster. We've all been through it, and we will help you through it."

"Let's get you cleaned up, then you should try to rest for a bit. It sounds like you've had a long, rough trip. A good night's sleep will work wonders."

The ladies helped me up from the bathroom floor, gave me a glass of water, and guided me to my room.

"We'll shut the door and let you change; take a nap, or whatever you need. If you want company, just open it. We'll be here." Doris' motherly charm eased my wobbly stomach.

After the door was shut, I changed into yoga pants and a t-shirt. I then snuck back into the bathroom to brush my teeth. I saw Janice in the hallway on my way there. I held up my brush and toothpaste to signify my purpose; she winked, and went on her way.

I crawled into the small, yet comfy bed and fell asleep within seconds. My mind and body were exhausted. I slept for several hours before waking up in a panic. I saw Rick's body, lying lifeless on his back deck. It was surrounded by crusty, burgundy blood. I remembered the money the moment I woke up from that vivid image.

Unfortunately, Maya and Katelyn were now asleep in their beds. I couldn't turn the light on. I also didn't want to move around a lot and risk waking either of them. I spent the rest of the night unable to sleep, wishing I was in Esteban's bed and that the last week was just a horrific nightmare.

As soon as the sun came up, I reached for the suitcase. I had tucked it under my bed after I grabbed the clothes I was sleeping in. I was so overwhelmed with emotion last night that despite opening my suitcase and being reminded of the money mere moments prior, I didn't take two seconds to confirm no one had taken any.

I slowly unzipped the case, trying to make as little sound as possible. The other two women appeared oblivious to any noise I was making. I lifted the lid and checked each hiding spot, all of which appeared untouched. I couldn't count it, but I felt confident the kind nature of these women was more sincere than most people. I zipped it back up, sighed, and settled back inside the soft, reassuring bedding.

I must have fallen asleep again; when I woke up the next time, Maya was no longer in the room and Katelyn was sitting up, reading in her bed. I'm usually not a sound sleeper, and was surprised their movement hadn't woken me sooner.

"Good morning, Katelyn."

"Good morning, Pam. How did you sleep? I hope we didn't wake you."

"Not at all. I didn't even hear Maya get up."

"She went to take a shower a few minutes ago. There's only one shower, and it's on a first-come, first-served basis."

"Hmmm. I'm not so worried about showering, but I do need to pee, like now." My voice sounded whiny and entitled, so I immediately added, "Sorry, I can wait until she's done. I understand we need to share the facilities here."

"There's a second washroom downstairs. It just doesn't have a tub or shower in it."

"Thank you! I didn't mean to come off demanding."

"No worries; when you've got to pee, you've got to pee." Katelyn teased.

I expected the rest of the house to still be sleeping, but Donna, Doris, and Suzanne were already awake and preparing breakfast in the kitchen. I quietly snuck past them and went downstairs to use the extra bathroom. Fortunately, it was not occupied.

Waking up in a strange house surrounded by women I don't know had me on edge. Although they seemed too nice to be true, I didn't feel like I had made a very good first impression. I was nervous about approaching them after the way last night ended, so I stayed in the washroom a few extra minutes to collect myself. I reassured myself that they didn't seem judgmental last night, and it was doubtful they would be now. I took a deep breath, opened the door, and went straight to the kitchen.

"Good morning. Can I help you with breakfast?" I was relieved that I could talk without my voice shaking.

"Everything is just about ready. We serve breakfast more like a buffet, since we don't all get up at the same time. You can put out some plates, forks, and spoons for everyone," Doris said while pointing to the cupboards where they were kept.

"Sure!"

I was grateful for the simplicity of the task. My stomach was still twisted with nerves and guilt. I felt like a fraud amongst saints. I quickly but cautiously set the table. Suzanne put out a basket of homemade blueberry muffins, a big bowl of cut strawberries, and a tub of Greek yogurt. Donna was making hard-boiled eggs, and Doris had just finished putting on a pot of coffee.

"Everyone has different eating habits early in the morning, so we have a lot of options. There's bread and bagels next to the toaster, a few kinds of cereal in that cupboard, and more eggs in the fridge if you want to make yourself one your way." Doris pulled a bunch of mismatched mugs from the cupboard above the coffee maker and placed them in front of it as she spoke. "Donna and I like hard-boiled eggs, so she always makes a few of those."

"I don't usually eat much this early. The muffin and strawberries are plenty."

"Please, help yourself. I'm just waiting on the coffee. I can't function without it!"

"That's a necessity for me too!"

I waited until Suzanne fixed her plate, and then grabbed a muffin and a few strawberries. I took a seat at the far end of the table, while Suzanne decided to stand next to Doris and the brewing pot of coffee. Maya came into the kitchen and greeted everyone with a cheerful good morning. She took a muffin and plopped down in the seat across from me.

"How did you sleep, Pam?" Maya asked while she picked at the fluffy baked good. Her hair was still in a towel on top of her head.

"Surprisingly, I slept really well. I'm not normally comfortable sleeping in unfamiliar places, but I crashed pretty fast."

"Exhaustion is your body's way of making sure you get the rest it needs," Donna chimed in.

"I was more tired then I realized," I replied, quickly followed by, "these muffins are incredible! Who made them?"

"Angie made the batter this morning before going to the diner. She took two dozen with her, and left enough for me to make a dozen. We make muffins a lot because they're cheap, easy, and profitable," Suzanne joined in the conversation.

My inner confusion must have been apparent on my face, because Doris picked up where Suzanne left off.

"We're very fortunate a local diner helps us afford food in a few different ways. We sell the muffins for $1.50 at his diner, and get to keep the entire profits. He also lets any of the women here work there in exchange for food. Many of the women who stay here don't want bank accounts or their Social Insurance Number linked to the area, so the work they do is viewed as volunteering and the food is given as a donation."

Suzanne continued, "Bill's really nice, and will let you eat for free while you work, plus he lets you take $10 worth of groceries for every hour you work."

Maya added, "When you waitress, you can make really great tips. It's nice being able to earn some money."

Doris said, "His daughter was killed while trying to leave her abusive husband four years ago. They've donated kitchen supplies, held fundraisers, and did a canned food drive on our behalf. Bill and his wife Debbie are always willing to help out so we can keep this place running."

What a remarkable, generous couple to have turned their tragedy into something beautiful, I thought. The only word that made its way from my lips was, "Wow."

"If you're interested in working there, we'll fit you into that schedule, too. We try to keep things fair, having everyone take turns between waitressing shifts and working in the kitchen, Doris continued.

I loved the idea of doing something to pay these women back for opening their home and hearts to me. "I'm not much of a cook, but I can waitress."

"We'll teach you how to cook. Everyone prefers the waitressing shifts, so you have to take turns," Doris responded sternly.

"Oh, sure, of course," I mumbled.

"Cooking at the diner is easy; it's mostly slap it on the grill or drop it in the deep-fryer. If I can cook it, anyone can!" Maya reassured me.

I gave her a gracious smile and then focused my attention on my plate. I was hoping to divert their attention away from me. I felt certain that becoming a member of this household was going to force me to step outside of my comfort zone. I was willing to try new experiences; I just doubted my abilities to succeed without looking like a fool.

"I'll work on the schedules after breakfast, and we'll help you through the adjustment period." Doris came over and rubbed my shoulder gently. It felt like she could read my mind. "Janice should be stopping by shortly, if you need to chat."

I mumbled a thank you, and slowly finished the last few crumbs of the delicious homemade muffin. I couldn't look her in the eye to show how much I truly appreciated her patience with me. I felt guilty that I wasn't the victim of abuse I pretended to be.

I hadn't realized that Janice didn't sleep there like everyone else. I later discovered she was a practicing psychologist with her own home office, about fifteen minutes away. She was a former victim of abuse who spent most of her free time volunteering at the shelter. Her only son had moved to London, Ontario after university, which is also where her ex lives. Since she was single and lived alone, she had a lot of spare time, love, and advice to give.

I finished my breakfast, put the plate in the sink with the others, and fixed myself a coffee. I stood there silently drinking it, listening to the other women discuss the diner's menu, their plans for the day, and daily duties that I had yet to partake in.

Despite how inviting and understanding everyone was behaving, I still felt awkward and out of place. My gut kept insisting that my dishonesty about the circumstances that brought me here was the reason I didn't belong with this group of strong survivors.

Technically, I'm just as much of a victim of abuse as these women. I've been in several relationships that turned ugly. Men have hit me, smacked me, and torn into my self-esteem to the extent I felt worthless. I thought I had overcome being victimized until I met Esteban, and then Rick. They were proof that I was still a sucker for smooth-talking men. I had repeated my mistakes even though my past had taught me ways to protect myself, to keep myself from falling victim again. There was still a lesson I had yet to learn.

I was still lost in my thoughts when I realized the other women had begun to clean up the continental breakfast spread. Once again, I wanted to feel useful—but wasn't sure how to merge myself into their fluid movements. Everyone seemed to know where to put things and what their role was in the kitchen. I handed my now empty mug to Maya, who had already begun washing the dishes in the sink. I quickly scanned the room, looking for something I could do.

I plucked two crumpled napkins off the table and put them in the garbage. That was all the help I could be, since everything else was cleaned up within a matter of seconds. I was suddenly looking forward to being on the chore schedule so I would know exactly what I could do to contribute to this household.

Fortunately, it didn't take long for Doris to revise and post a new schedule. I'm not sure if Doris could detect my lack of domesticity, but she assigned me the easiest chores possible. I had lunchtime dish washing duty, setting the table for dinner, and vacuuming the basement carpet on Sundays. However, she did block off an hour after vacuuming on Sundays for me to assist her with dinner. I figured it would be a good opportunity for me to learn more about cooking without the pressure of being responsible for the outcome of the meal. I'm sure this was Doris' logic, as well.

She took me aside later and said she would put me on the diner schedule the following week, once I felt more comfortable. As much as I wanted to contribute financially, I agreed with her recommendation. I also had money of my own and an overwhelming urge to give every cent of it to these women.

Sheltered from the Past

The next few days flew by. The other women taught me their techniques for passing time in captivity. The shelter had a massive bookcase filled with donated books, board games, and puzzle books that everyone shared. Donna knitted, Suzanne painted, and the rest of the women fussed over the garden. There was also a grade school with a one mile track about a block away, where I went running with Katelyn and Maya before lunch each day.

I would usually spend twenty or thirty minutes a day alone with Janice, as well. I was still vague with the details, and did my best to skirt the truth without directly lying. The other women shared bits and pieces of their toxic relationships, but didn't pry into mine. They were each at different stages of their healing process, and were not overly open or descriptive when it came to what they endured. I figured my guarded behavior suited the profile.

The first person besides Janice to ask me about my abusive ex was Angie, on the fourth night I stayed at the house. We were playing Euchre after dinner with Donna and Suzanne. We'd just won the third out of four games, and decided to call it a night. Donna was headed to bed, and Suzanne wanted to watch TV with the rest of the women.

"They're watching *Real Housewives*. I can't watch spoiled women argue and fight over nothing," Angie commented, after Suzanne left the table.

"Not really my thing either."

My shyness had worn off, and I found it very easy to talk to all the women there. I wasn't internally stressing over if they were judging or doubting me anymore. Within a matter of days, my comfort level had grown rapidly. It felt so much like home that the nightmare-inspiring flashbacks from the week before had completely stopped.

"I'm not tired yet, either. Do you want to have a tea, and maybe sit in the backyard?"

"That sounds like a great idea."

We put on the kettle, made a bag of microwave popcorn, and both threw on a sweater, since the sun had set hours earlier. We settled into two padded patio chairs. The view in front wasn't anything spectacular, but the view above sparkled with wonder and possibilities.

"I like coming out here at night; gives me a chance to think." Angie was also staring at the sky scattered with tiny stars. "I prefer to keep busy during the day, to distract myself from reliving the last few years with my ex. I can still clearly picture every awful incident. The memory and pain is as fresh as if it was yesterday."

I gave the top of her hand a gentle pat, but didn't know what I should say.

"It's been almost three months since I left my husband. I still haven't figure out where I'm supposed to go from here. Sorry, I should sound more hopeful. I just thought I'd be over it by now."

"It's okay. I'm not ready to be hopeful myself. I have no clue how to build a real life again."

Angie chuckled. "A real life? Not even sure what that would be. This place has become very real to me; I can't imagine ever leaving it."

There was a four- or five-minute silence while we both let reality sink in. We felt safe and cared for at the shelter, but it wasn't meant to be a forever home. Eventually, we would each need to take ownership of our future and venture into the real world. We'd have to figure out a way to survive without Doris and Janice looking out for us. I was only in their all-encompassing care for a few days, and it felt like the lifeline I'd been searching for since the first time my mother shared the revolting story of my conception.

"I know I'll have to move out one day. Janice has her own place, even though she's here almost every day. Tanya left about a week before you showed up. She came back the next day to visit for a few hours, and hasn't been back since. I'm pretty sure I'll be more like Janice. The women here are like family to me."

The closeness and genuine concern amongst the women was obvious. They acted like family with each other, and had already earned their place as friends in my heart. It was similar to the bond I'd had with the other dancers at Planet Hollywood, except with a lot less sparkly cleavage and petty drama. It was also very different because my fellow dancers knew my real name.

"Does your family know you're here, Pam?" Angie asked innocently.

"No."

"Do you worry about them? Have any children? I already consider you a good friend, yet I know so little about you."

Oh, no. Here we go. My new friend wants to know more about me and I have no choice other than to lie to her. I hadn't Googled the local or American news since I arrived; I had to be careful not to say anything to connect me with either case. Rick's body must have been found by now.

The thought of Rick's bloody face sent shivers down my spine.

"I don't have any children, and I'm not really close with my family." I thought about how much my grandma would be worrying over my sudden disappearance.

"Do you think your ex will find you here?"

I turned my hands palms up and shrugged, knowing Esteban wouldn't be turning up anytime soon.

"How long were you with your ex?"

"A little more than a year. He was so romantic in the beginning, but it went downhill quickly." I was lying about how long I had been with Esteban, but the rest of what I said was true. I didn't want to admit that I blindly trusted a man after only knowing him for a couple of weeks.

"It's the charming guy they pretend to be in the beginning that makes us such fools for them." Angie said with a serious scowl. "I grew up in a good home, did well in school, and got a great job right after college. I thought meeting Dave was the last piece of the puzzle. I never thought I'd be dumb enough to fall for a manipulative asshole; yet here I am."

Silence.

"Sorry, we're not fools. You're not a fool, or dumb. I just never thought my life would take me here."

"Me neither."

We sat there in silence, staring at the sky until our mugs and popcorn bowl were empty. I was starting to realize that I wasn't the only lost soul who had ended up here. All the women staying at the shelter had similar stories, their lives being twisted upside down because they fell for the wrong guy.

As I got to know the women, I began to see their resilience and determination. They were proud they'd left their awful exes, excited to learn new skills, and ready to live better lives. It was inspiring to be around them. They were so kind and helpful to one another that it made me want to be a better person. Doris created a loving, supportive environment that everyone appreciated.

Within days of knowing her I wished Doris had been my mother. She spent four hours cooking and baking with me the first Sunday I was at the house. She explained every step, and told funny stories from her past that made her laugh, a hopelessly contagious belly laugh. We started by making a simple banana bread, which was easier than I ever imagined. We then made lasagna, garlic bread, and green beans with almonds.

She then gave me a lesson on cooking eggs, since my first shift at the diner was the following morning. Angie had already agreed to work with me, but I didn't want to look like a fool in front of her. Doris completely understood.

"I don't want to waste any eggs, but can you explain how to cook the different types? I want to be useful with Angie tomorrow, and the only eggs I've ever made are scrambled."

"Of course, my dear! We can make one of each type, and serve it to everyone as an appetizer."

It was fun cooking with Doris, and just as great the next morning with Angie. She made the eggs for the first hour, while I managed toast, bacon, and sausages. Then she let me try, while she guided me. Like Doris, Angie had a patient way of explaining things that made it easy.

After only two weeks, these women had become my world. I was fighting a nagging pain that I would need to run somewhere else one day, but still happier than I'd been since Esteban was killed. I was building the new life I so desperately needed.

Unfortunately, the chance of my cover being blown increased drastically the week after my first shift at the diner. It was my first successful solo breakfast shift in the kitchen, and I was feeling proud of being able to keep up with all the orders. I was feeling so confident about my new skills that I volunteered to help with both lunch and dinner. It's amazing how quickly something that I was fearful of learning had turned into something I loved to do.

Doris, Donna, Suzanne, and Angie were in the living room watching the news after dinner, while I was sitting in the kitchen chatting with Maya and Katelyn about their plans to go back to college. Janice had asked me about going back to school in our last session. I had more than enough money in the suitcase to pay for it, but zero ideas as to what program I should take.

"I wanted to be a nurse, but I just don't think my stomach could handle it. I also get emotional pretty easily. I need an easier career where I can still help people," Maya explained.

"I was hoping to become a teacher, but there just doesn't seem to be a demand around here. Two of my friends became teachers, and neither has been able to find full-time work," Katelyn lamented.

I was listening to their conversation when I saw Suzanne run from the living room. She went into her room and quickly slammed the door shut. That silenced both Maya and Katelyn long enough for me to hear the story they were watching on the news.

"Three bodies were found today in the backyard of murder victim, Richard Thompson." The newscaster announced, before turning the microphone over to a Leamington police officer.

"Mr. Thompson was reported missing five days ago, by a coworker. We discovered his last known whereabouts was O'Neil's Irish Pub in Windsor. The bartender overheard him offering his cottage to a young woman with a suitcase. When we investigated the cottage, we found Mr. Thompson bludgeoned to death on his back deck. After searching the residence, we discovered items belonging to three missing persons. Today we uncovered the bodies of those three women, buried in Mr. Thompson's backyard. Mr. Thompson's killer is still unknown at this time. If anyone has additional information on the woman who was last seen with Mr. Thompson, please contact police immediately. She appears to be in her mid-twenties and is described as five foot seven, approximately a hundred and thirty pounds, with long blonde hair."

I'm actually 5'8" and closer to 150 pounds, but I knew that wasn't enough to divert suspicion. My heart was pounding so loud that I didn't hear anything else the news had to say about the case. It pounded even louder when I saw Doris looking over her shoulder, through the entranceway to the kitchen, directly at me. I couldn't see my reflection, but felt certain I wasn't hiding the panic welling up inside of me.

"Is Suzanne okay?" Katelyn asked, as she got up from the table and went into the living room.

"Richard Thompson is her ex-husband." Doris said softly as she got up from her seat. "I'll go check on her."

"Wow," was all Maya could say.

I sat motionless, soaked in sweat, debating whether I should grab my suitcase and run. I could faintly hear the other women discussing the shock and horror of the situation. They were worried about how Suzanne would take the news of his death, and more frightening, the implication of bodies buried in his backyard.

It's selfish and I can admit it, but the only person I was worried about was me. I fit the description of the last woman seen with him. I had arrived at the house the following day with a suitcase and told Doris I crossed into Canada at a border city. I was pretty sure I never mentioned being in Windsor to any of the women at the shelter, but that wouldn't be enough to counteract the other similarities. She was staring at me before she went to check on Suzanne. My gut was screaming that Doris knew all my dirty secrets.

Doris and Suzanne came out of the bedroom a few minutes later, both of their eyes puffy from crying. All the other women in the house instantaneously ended their discussions, turning their attention and sympathetic eyes towards Suzanne.

"Suzanne and I are going to take a drive to see Janice." Doris advised us, and the two women hurried towards the door.

"We'll be here for you when you get back," Maya called out.

"We love you, Suzie Q!" Angie said, as tears welled in her eyes.

Katelyn waved and Donna blew her a kiss as the door shut behind them. I was still motionless and silent. I felt like my legs had locked in place. The other four were standing in the front room, just on the other side of the kitchen entrance. I wanted to join them, to blend in, but I couldn't get up from the table.

"I can't imagine how she feels," Donna said softly.

"You'd think you would want to celebrate your ex's death, after all the hell he put you through. It's just not the case, though. As much as we want to hate them, the love is still there," Angie said, staring at the closed door.

"There's no love left for my ex. I feel like I could celebrate his death," Maya firmly stated.

"I couldn't," Angie stated softly.

"I could," Katelyn whispered.

I was the only one who didn't comment. My ex was dead, and I was the woman responsible for Suzanne's ex-husband's death. My frozen, sweaty, shaking body was pinned to the kitchen chair.

"Doris and Janice will help her process her emotions. She'll be okay," Donna reassured the group.

We shared a few minutes of silence before everyone wandered off their separate ways. Donna went to her room, Katelyn went to ours, and Angie slipped outside. Maya sat down on the couch and started flipping through the channels. I didn't want to strike up a conversation with anyone, so I stayed by myself at the kitchen table.

I started the familiar process of creating a cover story and getaway plan, in case I was confronted. As of right now, there was no direct threat to my freedom. I had time to develop a way out of my current mess. I needed to go online so I could research other border crossings, in case I was questioned. I felt pretty certain there was a bridge between New York and Niagara Falls, but I had no idea where Niagara Falls was compared to my current location. I thought I'd seen a sign for it when I was driving to Toronto.

The shelter didn't have internet service, probably for security reasons. There was an old computer in the basement with Microsoft Office programs for creating resumes or other writing projects. The women went to a nearby library to use their internet, if they needed to research something. These women were in hiding, so they had no interest in checking their Facebook or Twitter. I was the same way. I had created profiles, but very rarely used them to interact with people. I certainly wasn't going to check my old accounts now.

I need to do a lot of research. It had been days since I checked in on the case of missing Samantha Tilson or Esteban's murder. I also wanted to know if the police had any leads on Richard's murder, or if they knew the most-likely deceased Allison McFarland checked into a Toronto hotel the night of his murder. I had to map out a timeline that explained the details I'd shared so far without mimicking any part of Samantha Tilson's past, or that of the woman who had just murdered Suzanne's ex-husband.

My palms were sweating, my vision was blurry, and my body shook uncontrollably. I wasn't crying, yet I felt like I couldn't catch my breath. The more I thought about the horrific events I was trying to cover up, the more my stomach roiled. I was tired of scamming my way out of mistake after mistake—so tired that I must have passed out.

I woke up a few hours later, neatly tucked into my bed at the shelter. I couldn't remember how I got there, and it took me a few minutes to remember why I had a panic attack. I had been on the run for over two weeks; my past was catching up with me, and I finally realized the only choice I had left was to tell the truth.

My stomach muscles clenched at the mere thought of what that would imply. In the case of Richard, it would be easy to claim self-defense, followed by panic. As for fleeing with Esteban's money, I still had most of it, and could turn it in to the police. The consequences wouldn't be that bad. Maybe I could even get my job back at Planet Hollywood.

The thought of going back to Vegas didn't inspire the smile I thought it would. Instead, I was thinking what a loss it would be to lose these women. I had so much respect and appreciation for their kindness and support. Once the truth came out, I knew they'd lose respect for me.

How could they support me, knowing I was responsible for Suzanne's ex-husband's death? In the words of Angie: "As much as we want to hate them, the love is still there." Suzanne bursting into tears at the news of his death was proof she still had love for him.

I was lying in my bed, pondering how to be truthful and not hated by these women, when Katelyn peeked in to check on me.

"You're awake!" She exclaimed. "We were worried about you. How are you feeling?"

I managed to squeak out "Okay," although that wasn't how I felt. I felt guilty they are worrying about me when they should be concerned with Suzanne's situation.

"Do you want something to drink or eat?"

"No, I'm fine. Thank you."

"Suzanne just came back. We're in the living room talking, if you feel up to it," Katelyn said with a sympathetic smile.

I nodded, and a felt a tight lump form in my throat. There was no way I could admit to everything that happened in front of Suzanne, especially today. I knew the right thing to do was suck it up, go out there, and be supportive. I waited for Katelyn to close the door, then sat up and took a few deep breaths. I was ready to act like a good person before I confessing that I wasn't, really.

When I approached the living room, the women were all snuggled around Suzanne. Her head was resting on Doris's shoulder. I hung a few feet back and then slowly slid into the room. I didn't want to take the attention away from Suzanne.

"At least I don't have to worry about him ever hurting me again," Suzanne said quietly.

"Yes, it's a good thing you left when you did," Doris replied.

"I couldn't imagine still being with him and discovering he was so much worse than I thought. How could I love a rapist and murderer for so many years?"

"We've all made bad choices in men. The more evil the man, the more cunning his game," Janice said, giving Suzanne's hand a gentle squeeze.

"Richard was pure evil. I took me time to see it, but I know it now. If some woman he tried to rape or kill did this to him, he deserved it. I can't believe I'm saying it, but he deserved to die." She started to cry heavy sobs as soon as the last word slipped out. So did I.

Doris wrapped her arms around Suzanne, rubbed her back, and kept repeating, "Let it out, my dear. Let it out, my love."

As I was wiping tears from my chin, I noticed Maya, Katelyn, and Angie were also crying. Everyone sobbed silently while Suzanne wailed loudly in Doris's arms. After a few minutes of letting it out, Doris decided it was time to refocus our energy.

"Okay, ladies. We're survivors and as horrible as this is, Suzanne will survive. We'll be here to make sure of it. Now, it's getting late and we all need a good night's sleep."

"I'm going to spend the night. Is there a spare bed in your room?" Janice asked Suzanne, who was surfacing from her nestling spot in Doris's chest.

Suzanne shook her head no. Angie piped in, "I'm in the same room, but I'll sleep somewhere else if she wants you with her."

"I'm fine, Janice. Angie can stay. I've talked enough. I just want to sleep."

"There's a spare bed in my room, Janice," Doris offered.

"Great! I'll be there, if anyone needs me."

The women parted ways and all headed straight for bed. It was an emotional day for everyone, and I heard both Maya and Katelyn softly snoring within minutes of lying down. I couldn't sleep. Once again, my mind was racing, my stomach was turning, and I was fighting back tears with everything I had in me.

Suzanne said Richard deserved it. I had been trying to reassure myself since the incident that what I did to him was justified. If a woman who once loved him could accept that he was responsible for his ill fate, then I could too. *Hopefully she's still as understanding when she learns I was the last woman he tried to rape.*

Morning Confessions

I must have fallen asleep at some point, although it felt like I tossed and turned for most of the night. When I woke up, the sun had just started to rise. Both of my roommates were still peacefully sleeping. I decided to sneak in a shower before the morning rush. I gathered my clothes, quietly made my way to the washroom, and enjoyed a long, hot shower. When I was finished, I went into the kitchen to get the first pot of coffee started. Before I reached the entrance, I could sense someone beat me to it. The smell of brewing coffee was quickly filling the house.

"Good morning." Doris greeted me before I noticed her.

"Good morning! I was going to make coffee, but smells like you already did."

"I'm an early riser. I get up with the sun, like clockwork."

"I didn't sleep well last night."

"Something weighing on your mind?" Doris raised her eyebrow and gave me a look like she already knew the answer. I completely forgot about her staring at me when the news was first broadcast.

"I just feel so bad for Suzanne."

"Are you worried your ex could behave the same way?"

"Possibly... Maybe, but that's not everything on my mind." I took a deep breath and decided Doris was the person to confide in. "There's so much I need to say, but there are so many fears forcing me to hold it inside."

Those familiar knots ripped at my stomach once again. Living this lie was making me ill; I couldn't do it anymore. I looked up to a god who I'd never confided in before, and begged for the strength to be honest for the first time in forever. Tears were streaming down my cheeks, making it difficult to speak. That's when Doris said, "Let it out, my love."

I kept my focus an inch above her forehead and released the torrid tale of my journey here. Every detail poured out like a rapid waterfall. I explained how and why I fell in love with Esteban, witnessed his murder, took off with the case full of money, and the deadly encounter with Suzanne's former husband.

I didn't break once to take more than a gasping breath or choke back my tears. I let it out in one lump sum, expecting to see horror transform Doris's motherly smile into shame or anger. She rubbed my back, squeezed my hand, and kept her reassuring smile the entire time.

"Once I realized he wasn't moving, I panicked. I cleaned the place of any trace that I was there, stole his keys, and drove to Toronto. His Explorer is parked in a garage downtown somewhere. That's when I decided to come here."

I exhaled and slumped forward, drained, as the last words were confessed. Despite the consequences I'd just exposed myself to, I told Doris it felt a like a weight had been lifted.

"Well, I'm glad. We'll help you through it, Pam."

"That's the worst part. Everyone here has been so kind and supportive. I don't deserve it. I'm a fraud. My real name isn't even Pam. It's Samantha Tilson."

"It's nice to finally meet you, Samantha."

I blushed when she said my full name.

"You didn't ask for the circumstances that put you here to happen, but it brought you to the right place. All the women here found themselves in situations beyond their control. We have legal connections, support groups, and counselors who will help you deal with this mess. The first and hardest step is admitting it."

I managed to whisper "Thank you," as a few tears trembled down my cheek.

"I'm sorry you've been through so much. I can't imagine what the last few weeks must have felt like. I've had my share of rough days, but nothing like what you experienced."

I knew a little about Doris's story. She had shared a few things as examples of what a person can endure and overcome. She had been married for 23 years when her husband lost his job. He started drinking heavily, refused to work, and began to belittle her on a daily basis. Within a year, it escalated to him throwing things at her—then he smacked her so hard she fell down a flight of stairs and broke her leg.

Her wake-up happened instantly, because her older son saw her injuries in the hospital. When he realized his father had caused it, he insisted that she leave him. Doris moved in with her son, regained her independence and later opened the shelter.

Doris's story of abuse wasn't as tragic as most of the things I'd picked up on in the house. I knew Katelyn's ex-boyfriend had set her on fire. She had a few noticeable burns and a sincere fear of fire. That's why she didn't work at the diner. Maya's ex-boyfriend had hit her often, and it took five years before she had the courage to leave.

"Thank you. My life hasn't been easy, but the last few weeks have obviously been more than I can handle."

"That's why you've been getting sick and passing out. You have all this stress and anxiety building up inside of you. It's manifesting in physical symptoms."

I nodded. I felt certain she was right.

"I feel a little better now that I told someone."

"Do you want to tell the rest of the house? I hear some noise down the hall and it's just about the time everyone starts waking up."

"I don't know, probably not. I'm worried about Suzanne's reaction."

"Okay; for today, this is just between us. I think Suzanne is going to need all of us. Take the day to recover, and have faith that this is a temporary problem. You'll have a team to help you solve it tomorrow."

"Thank you so much." Tears were starting to form again, but I could hear Angie and Suzanne coming towards the kitchen. I quickly wiped my face and forced a smile.

"Good morning!" Doris cheerfully greeted the pair.

Angie smiled. Suzanne looked somber and defeated. Neither said anything. The breakfast gathering was quieter than normal. The only sounds were sizzling bacon, coffee brewing, dishes clanging, and the occasional polite chit-chat about the weather. The other women could tell Suzanne needed to wallow, and let her establish the tone of the meal.

Janice invited Suzanne and Doris into her office immediately after breakfast, and the remaining women started cleaning up the kitchen. Katelyn was the first one to break the funeral home whispers we had recently adapted.

"I've got a great idea!" Katelyn exclaimed, pumping her fist in the area. "Let's take Suzanne for a nature walk: the same place where we saw that deer."

She must have noticed the look of confusion on our faces, because she immediately added, "I know it's off topic, but I was wondering what we could do to break her funk and it just came to me. I know being outdoors helps me."

"It's a wonderful idea," Angie quickly reassured her.

"I would love to go, but I'm already late for work. I think Suzanne is on the schedule as well," Maya advised.

"I can take Suzanne's shift," I eagerly volunteered. It was the least I could do, since I was responsible for her sorrow. I quickly added, "And she can have any tips I make."

"Great! That's so nice of you!" Donna praised me.

"It's the least I can do." I confessed with more conviction than any of those women realized—except Doris, of course. I raced to our room, quickly changed, and left for the diner with Maya. I secretly thought it would be easier not having to face Suzanne in front of Doris, now that I had confessed.

After a brief closed-door chat, Katelyn, Angie, Suzanne, and Janice decided to go for a walk while Doris and Donna agreed to stay back to prepare lunch and dinner. When I impulsively volunteered to take Suzanne's shift waitress, I forget I had the dinner shift in the kitchen as well. The owner would be working with me, and I was little nervous about it up until I heard the more disturbing news on TV the day before.

Maya attempted to start some idle chit-chat on our walk to the diner, but my mind wasn't absorbing any of it. I was still stunned by Doris' reaction to the truth. I admitted to witnessing a murder, running from the scene of the crime with a suitcase full of cash, fleeing the country, and then killing

Suzanne's ex-husband. Although killing him was obviously self-defense, I had just confessed to several serious crimes.

The diner was slower than usual that morning, so my thoughts had plenty of time to wander. I momentarily panicked when I realized I left the suitcase (money) at the house and Doris now knew it existed. I calmed my fears quickly; Doris was an unlikely thief. I was also worried she'd change her mind and call the authorities, but that was doubtful too. I believed all the kind things she said after my confession.

My waitressing shift ended at three, which was exactly when Angie showed up to take over. I had a thirty-minute break before I was expected to handle the dinner rush with the owner. I spent it sipping coffee while picking at a plate of fries. I was nervous, but determined. Working in that diner gave me a way to pay Doris back for her kindness and generosity. I forced myself to forget about Rick, Suzanne, and my confession to Doris. Cooking for the customers required my full attention.

"Are you ready?" Bill asked with a warm smile.

"As ready as I'll ever be!" I said, with all the enthusiasm I could muster.

"Okay, let's go over tonight's specials and how we'll divide the menu before it gets busy," Bill said, as he went through the swinging doors into the tiny kitchen. I followed and listened intently as he advised me of what items I would be responsible for preparing, and what we needed to prep in advance. He knew I wasn't an experienced cook, so he assigned me all of the side dishes, salads, and desserts. Once I started working, everything went smoothly. I completely forgot about the mess I would have to face tomorrow.

When the last table was served and cleared, Bill let me pick out $150 worth of groceries, even though I had only worked thirteen hours. He knew why I took Suzanne's shift, and said I deserved a little extra for being such a good person. He obviously didn't know that I was the person responsible for Suzanne's ex-husband's death.

It was almost ten o'clock when Angie and I got back to the house. Janice had gone home, Doris and Donna had retired to their bedroom for the night, and the remaining women were cuddled under a blanket on the couch watching TV.

"Thank you so much for taking my shift, Pam," Suzanne gushed when she saw me enter the living room. "I knew I'd never be able to focus on customers today. I am so grateful you volunteered to do it."

The combination of her appreciation and using the fake name twisted my stomach in knots.

"It was fine. Here's the tips I made this morning. You should keep them."

I pulled out the crumpled bills and change, totaling a measly $18.25. I tried to hand it to Suzanne, but she sat on her hands and shook her head adamantly.

"It was your shift, and you shouldn't lose out. Please, take it," I pleaded. I could feel tears forming in my eyes.

"Oh no, you earned that. You're keeping it. Didn't you just work thirteen hours? That's a long day, and you deserve every cent," Suzanne insisted.

Well, that was the last straw. My conscience was eating me alive. My body started to shake, and I felt like I was going to throw up all over Suzanne. Instead, I dropped the money on the blanket that covered her lap, screamed "I killed Rick!" and bolted out the front door as fast as humanly possible.

I'd slipped off my shoes when I first entered the house, but didn't bother to put them back on. I ran in my socks for two city blocks without stopping before tumbling onto some stranger's lawn. That's where the french fries and broccoli I'd munched on earlier decided to resurface.

I was trying to gain control over the violent vomiting and snotty tears that accompanied it when I realized I had been followed. Katelyn was running, and only a few feet away. I could see Angie, Suzanne, and Maya walking quickly behind her. I was lying in the puke-covered grass, trembling beyond my control. Although none of these women ever struck me as violent, I felt momentarily afraid that they were coming to attack me.

"Are you okay?" Katelyn called out as she approached.

I moved my head up and down to signify I was fine, but the disheveled sight of me told a different story. She rushed to my side and wrapped a comforting arm around my shoulder, completely ignoring the bits of broccoli in my hair. The other women followed suit.

It was the same compassionate reaction I'd received when I got sick at the house on my first day. They helped me up from the lawn, held my hand on the walk back to the house, and brought me a warm cloth to clean my face. Their words and actions showed genuine concern, and no one mentioned the murder I bluntly confessed to prior to running away.

"Do you want something to drink?" Maya asked.

"Water," was all I could force from my parched throat. Between the exhaustion of being on my feet for thirteen hours followed by running two blocks, and losing the little food I ate, I felt dizzy and weak. I didn't trust my legs to hold me any longer, so I lowered myself onto the bathroom floor.

"Are you okay? Do you want us to drive you to the hospital?" Suzanne asked, with sympathetic eyes.

I shook my head slowly, then reassured her, "I just needed to sit down."

We stared silently at each other, both empathetic to what the other was enduring. Katelyn and Angie had similar expressions. Maya quickly returned with the glass of water. I took a few sips, and assumed the women were waiting patiently for me to explain my earlier outburst. I closed my eyes, inhaled the less-than-fresh bathroom air, and exhaled loudly before beginning.

"I'm sorry, Suzanne. I met him at a bar while I was running from my ex. Well, to be completely honest, I was running from the men who killed my ex. Rick took me to the cottage; we had dinner and wine. He put something in the wine, because I started to feel lightheaded when I had only taken a couple of sips. He started touching me, and tried to take me inside the house. I had to do it," squeaked from my lips before I burst into tears once more.

"I am so sorry," were the first words from Suzanne's mouth, followed swiftly by a bear hug. The other women were tearing up over our embrace. We hugged and cried on the bathroom floor of the shelter for several minutes before Doris broke the silence. She had overheard the noise, and came out to see what was going on.

"Everything okay, ladies?" Doris asked, despite the women huddled around the bathroom sink, obviously not okay.

"I told them the truth."

"It looks like the conversation went okay?"

"Yes, it actually did."

Once again, the tension in my stomach begun to subside. Doris waved us out of the washroom, and then offered to make us all tea and cookies. The mood in the house instantly changed back into comfort and joy. We joked about how funny we must have looked, all crammed in the bathroom, and even Suzanne laughed. Before we decided to call it a night and go to sleep, I told the other women that my real name was Sam.

"I've always loved the name Samantha. It suits you," Katelyn commented.

"That's pretty smart, going with Pam when your real name is Sam," Angie added.

"Thank you. Everyone has been so good to me. I hated lying to everyone."

"I'm glad you finally introduced everyone to the real Sam. There was no reason to lie in the beginning. We don't judge each other here. Tomorrow, we will figure out this mess together. Now, let's all get some well-deserved rest!" Doris said with a wink.

We took turns giving each other good-night hugs, then retired to our separate beds. I slept like a baby, undisturbed and nightmare-free. I woke up with a renewed feeling of hope. Maybe there was still a chance for me to live a good life.

FINDING SAM AGAIN

"Good morning, Katelyn!" I said with a confident smile.

"Good morning, Sam. How did you sleep?"

Katelyn placed a bookmark between the pages of the story she was reading as she turned her attention towards me. Her usual warmth and concern shone from her baby blue eyes, despite the shocking news I had revealed the previous day. I could tell she still cared about me.

"Very well! I feel hopeful for the first time in ages. I'm also happy to be Sam again!"

"Well, I'm happy to hear that!" Katelyn replied.

After a bit of an awkward silence, we both decided to get up and join the other women in the kitchen. The usual breakfast routine went on without a word about my confession and current predicament. Doris waited until all the dishes and breakfast goodies were put away before addressing the other mess we needed to clean up.

"Okay, ladies! I hate to be the one issuing the reality check, but we can't postpone dealing with it any longer." Doris announced to the group before addressing me directly. "You and I are going to fill Janice and Donna in on what's going on, and then go to the police. The four of us will go with you. I'm not sure if you knew, but Donna has a strong legal background. She also knows an amazing attorney who's usually willing to take pro-bono cases."

"I worked as a legal secretary for over twenty years. I'm still very close with my boss, Chris, and she's passionate about domestic violence cases," Donna added.

"It's not exactly a case of domestic violence," I said, sheepishly.

"Let's go into Janice's office, so Sam can fill you in on the details." Doris interjected.

I heard Donna mumble "Sam?" before following us into Janice's office. I started from the beginning, and shared all the poor choices I'd made and insanity I had experienced in greater detail than my prior confessions. Janice and Donna asked questions throughout, so they could fully understand my situation and offer useful advice.

"Well, I don't think it's as bad as you're thinking. If you're willing to return what's left of the money, you'll probably only be charged with obstruction of justice for fleeing. Killing Richard should be a clear case of self-defense, considering they found other women buried in his backyard. You can significantly reduce any sentence if you're willing to testify against the men who killed Esteban," Donna explained, once I was done sharing my story.

I shook my head back and forth slowly, trying to imagine if I would have the courage to confront the killers in a courtroom. They were dangerous, connected men who would make it their mission to silence any potential witnesses. I wasn't sure I could be that strong.

"I know it's scary, but if you can identify the men who killed him, you can make a plea deal." Donna could see the fear in my eyes when she mentioned testifying.

"Think it over. Are you ready to go to the police?" Doris asked.

"I guess I am. No point dragging this out."

"I'll call Chris to see if she can go with us," Donna volunteered. "You'll need a lawyer for what happened with Suzanne's ex."

"Thank you so much. Unfortunately, once I hand over the cash I took, I won't have any left to pay the lawyer."

"Chris is financially secure and not motivated by money. Trust me. She'll want to help."

Donna called Chris, but she had appointments booked all morning. Donna suggested waiting for her, but I was too anxious. Now that the cat was out of the bag, I needed to know the consequences of my confessions. I had to tell the police while I was still brave enough to follow through with it. There was an internal battle raging inside me, and I had to fight off the urge to run again.

I packed the money back into its original case and tucked it with the rest of my limited belongings back inside my suitcase. I hugged the other women goodbye, and left with Donna and Janice. Doris decided to stay at the house with Suzanne, who was still struggling with her own loss. We rode the entire fifteen-minutes to the police station in silence. Not one word was said between us until I approached the reception area. Janice stood a few inches to my left, and Donna did the same on my right side. It felt like they were two cement pillars propping me up.

"I have information on two murders, and would like to talk to an officer," raced from my mouth the moment the man behind the counter looked in my direction. I had been rehearsing that sentence from the time I got inside the car, and was eager to blurt it out. I thought if I hesitated, I would chicken out.

"Two murders?" The attractive young officer raised his eyebrow questioningly. "I'll get a detective."

"Thank you," Janice responded on my behalf as she scooped my hand into hers. My palms were sweating and my legs felt like jelly. I was worried I was about to pass out. We waited motionlessly for a few minutes before the officer called for us to follow him. When he noticed I was dragging the suitcase behind me, he stopped and insisted on searching it. I opened it up, showed him the large bundles of cash, and explained that I would be turning the money over to the police. I could tell his curiosity had been further piqued.

The officer brought us into a small, cinderblock room with a long table, four chairs, and no windows. The outside of the police station was warm and inviting, with beautiful gardens and giant windows. This room looked like the typical interrogation room from every TV law drama I had ever seen. My anxiety kicked into overdrive, and my body began to shake nervously. I must have looked guilty.

"Take a deep breath," Donna whispered in my right ear.

"Have a seat, and Detective Ortiz will be with you in a moment." The officer left the room and shut the door quietly behind him. It literally felt like the walls were closing in on me.

"It's going to be okay, Sam. We'll be here the entire time," Janice reassured me while giving my hand a gentle squeeze. Donna nodded in agreement and rested her hand on my back. Although my legs felt weak, I didn't move towards one of the chairs. Instead, we stood there huddled together for several minutes, waiting for the door to re-open. We didn't have to wait very long.

"Good morning, ladies. My name is Detective Ortiz."

"Good morning. My name is Janice, this is Donna, and Samantha." Janice took the lead and tightened her grip on my hand. She could feel my body trembling. "Sam has some important information on the Richard Thompson murder, as well as an unrelated murder in the U.S."

All eyes turned towards me.

"Please have a seat, and we'll take this one crime at a time."

Detective Ortiz motioned to the chairs in front of us. The detective looked to be in his late fifties. He had graying hair, deep lines around his eyes, and a compassionate smile. Janice and Donna guided me into a chair before taking their own. As soon as I felt secure in my seat, the confession came pouring out.

"I killed Richard Thompson. I didn't mean to kill him. I thought he was going to kill me. He drugged me, and when I realized what had happened, I hit him with a shovel, twice."

The detective's eyebrows rose slightly, but his comforting smile remained. "Are you confessing to murder? Do you want a lawyer before we proceed?"

"I don't have a lawyer right now, although I think I'll be able to get one."

"She'll have a lawyer this afternoon. She just felt it was best to tell the police what she knew as quickly as possible, since both murder investigations are ongoing," Donna interjected.

"If you're confessing to murder, you will be charged with the crime. We can wait for your lawyer."

"I don't want to wait any longer. I'm ready."

"Why didn't you come forward sooner?" Detective Ortiz asked.

"I was scared. I met Richard running from a murder I witnessed in Las Vegas."

"How about you start from the beginning, so I can piece this mystery together?" The detective had kind eyes and a gentle tone, which made it easier to spill my guts.

I started the crazy story from the last day I saw Esteban. I explained what I saw from his boat in Vegas, the threatening texts, and how the men I saw on the dock that day had high-profile connections in the U.S. I told him about my experience with criminal police officers, the detective with the mustache, and why I felt I needed to run. I explained how I crossed into Windsor, met Richard, and went back to his cottage. I told the detective that I felt fuzzy after a few sips of wine, and could tell he was trying to drug me.

"My survival instincts must have kicked in. Everything happened so fast. I was feeling light-headed. Richard had scooped me up by the waist, and was walking me towards the house. By the way he was touching me earlier, I was convinced he intended to rape me. I saw the shovel leaning next to the door, so I grabbed it and swung it at his head. I've never done anything like that before. I'm not a violent person. I didn't mean to kill him; I'm not a murderer." Tears began to stream down my cheeks.

"You don't strike me as a murderer." The detective looked sincerely sympathetic. "I don't know much about the Thompson murder, but from what I've read, there's a good chance he was planning on hurting you. I believe that investigation is being handled by the Leamington police. I'll get in touch with them and see if we can arrange a meeting. You will be charged with his murder, but I wouldn't panic. Get ahold of your lawyer as soon as possible. It does sound like you acted in self-defense, but you'll need to prove that to a jury."

The compassionate detective let out a loud sigh and continued, "As for what you witnessed in Vegas, we'll have to touch base with the authorities who are working on that case. If the men responsible are as dangerous as you think, it shouldn't be hard to get witness protection first. You did the right thing coming forward." He got up from his chair, gave me a soft pat on the back, and left the room to make a few phone calls.

I let out a huge sigh of relief the moment the door closed behind him. My companions exhaled the same sound of relief, and all our shoulders slumped down like a massive weight had been lifted. I wasn't thrilled at the thought of witness protection or testifying against Esteban's murders, but anything was better than living on the run.

"You're very brave for coming forward," Janice reassured me.

"It will be easy to prove self-defense. Once we're done here, I'll try calling Chris again. She's a great lawyer, and I'm sure she'll be willing to help." Donna added.

"Thank you both. I don't think I'd have the guts to come forward if it wasn't for both of you and Doris. I could never have done this alone."

"You had the guts to confess everything to us. You did that on your own, and you would have managed this as well. We're just here to help you through it," Janice replied.

Detective Ortiz came back after about fifteen minutes with a plan. "I contacted the Leamington police, and they do want to speak with you as quickly as possible. We'll have you transferred there right away, so you can get that situation addressed. Unfortunately, I looked into the murder of Esteban Ramirez, and I am concerned that one might be a little trickier to walk away from. There's already a warrant for your arrest."

Janice and Donna's mouths dropped open in horror. I already knew the police were investigating me, so it didn't come as a surprise. However, I wasn't sure what exactly the warrant was for, so my level of fear superseded my lack of shock.

"Did you know there was a warrant out on you?" Detective Ortiz asked sternly. I knew it wouldn't benefit me later if I lied now, so I answered somewhat honestly.

"I didn't know the police were looking for me until I arrived in Windsor. I didn't see anything about a warrant for my arrest, not that it would have convinced me to turn myself in earlier. I did see photos online of several of the men who were there when Esteban was killed. I also saw photos of those same men with high-level members of the LVPD. One is a fucking detective! I didn't know who I could trust!"

My volume rose in a defensive scream. I was partially lying, since I knew the police had a photo of me before I crossed into Canada. However, I didn't know the police had my name until I was inside Canada, so I was being truthful for the most part. I was trying to save myself, and genuinely worried I was about to end up in jail.

"Are you certain you were not involved in any crime leading up to his murder, or involved in the murder itself?"

"Absolutely not."

"But you did flee with a briefcase full of cash?"

"Yes."

"That makes it a bit more complicated. I think we should address the local murder first, and then find out if you need to be extradited to the States to investigate that warrant."

My heart sank and the heavy weight of anxiety reappeared in my unstable stomach.

"Since you just confessed to a murder and there is a warrant out for your arrest, we'll have to take you into custody now. I'll arrange for a police escort to Leamington, so they can file charges, take your statement, and set a bail amount. After you're finished there, we'll have to contact the LVPD."

"Please don't. The LVPD is corrupt. I'll be dead the moment I'm back on American soil." I could feel tears forming, and was determined to fight another crying spree.

"Unfortunately, you're going to have to trust in your justice system unless you can find a Canadian lawyer willing to help you stateside. I still need to keep you in custody and confiscate the money."

"I'll call Chris again!" Donna exclaimed before excusing herself to make the call.

The next few minutes were a whirlwind of activity. The detective placed me in cuffs, booked my suitcase into evidence, and helped me get into the back of his police car. A young female officer got into the driver's side and a middle-aged officer got into the passenger side. The two carried on a casual conversation about the weather and local sports teams, never once acknowledging my presence as we drove down the same boring highway I'd traveled after escaping Rick's cottage.

My mind was racing with potential outcomes. Donna promised her old boss would get in touch with the Leamington police before I got there, but I wasn't convinced. Why would a woman who had never met me care about some American woman with an arrest warrant? I'd just surrendered the only money I had, and saw no feasible way to pay for a lawyer in the foreseeable future.

I was now handcuffed and trapped in a cop car. I couldn't run away and build a new life. I was going to be turned over to the LVPD, and I'd probably be dead within days. If they had illegal dealings with Esteban or his crew they'd be eager to cover it up, especially if the police were involved in the murder. Panic rose and I forced myself to swallow the urge to vomit once again.

Once we arrived in Leaminton, the officers helped me out of the police car and brought me into a friendly-looking interrogation room. The walls were painted a warm shade of taupe, and there was a small window in the back wall. One of the officers who had escorted me there uncuffed one wrist and re-cuffed it to the arm of the chair. They waited in silence until the officer in charge of the case arrived.

"Are you Samantha Tilson?" A portly, older man who was not in uniform asked after entering the room. The two officers who drove me to Leamington nodded, then slipped away without further introduction or comment.

"Yes."

"I'm told you were the last person seen with Richard Thompson. Is that correct?"

"Yes."

"I would like to take your statement of what occurred for our records. Are you ready to provide a sworn statement, or would you like to wait for your lawyer?"

"I'm ready to give it now."

"Are you sure you don't want to wait for your lawyer?"

"Yes, I'm not sure if I even have a lawyer."

The detective who had not yet introduced himself, advised me the discussion would be taped and asked me to begin whenever I was ready. I started the story from when I met him at the bar, and ended it with leaving his car in a Toronto parking garage. He informed me the car had already been recovered and swabbed for fingerprints. They also knew I had used one of Richard's victims' ID at the hotel.

"Why didn't you go to the police after you realized Mr. Thompson was dead?"

"I didn't know that he was dead until I heard it on the news two days ago. I grew up in Vegas. I don't trust the police. A cop raped my mom; that's how I was conceived. The LVPD are as crooked as the criminals. I figured it was the same here."

"Not trusting the police is not a great excuse for running from the scene of a murder. If you can't trust the police, who do you trust?"

"No one," I said sheepishly.

"Well, it does sound like it would be self-defense. I wish I could close this part of my investigation, so we can focus on the real victims. However, we still have to charge you with his death and the fact you left him to die isn't going to work in your favor. Considering the more heinous crimes Mr. Thompson committed, your lawyer should be able to get you quickly released on bail. We've now discovered Mr. Thompson was responsible for the rape of six women and he killed four, all within the last six months. Your actions and confession will help give those victims and their families some closure."

I nodded unenthusiastically. I was still far away from getting any closure on the mess I was in.

"In my mind, you killed someone who was at the beginning of a serial murder spree. That tells me you're brave and able to make tough decisions under pressure. So, let's go back to why you ran after this happened. Why was I advised there's an arrest warrant out for you stateside?"

"I was already on the run when it happened. I didn't know there was an arrest warrant for me, but I knew the LVPD wanted to speak with me."

"Now we're getting somewhere. Let's start from the beginning of this mess."

I told the story of Esteban's murder yet again, making sure to stress why I felt I needed to flee the country. Once I connected the timeframe between the two murders together, I started to beg the detective to grant me witness protection before shipping me back to the States.

"Please, I've seen pictures of Esteban with the killers and the police. I know there's a connection. I'll be executed before there's even a trial."

"Hmmm. Let me look into that, and see exactly why there is a warrant for your arrest. I think a lawyer called earlier to verify you were being transferred here. Your lawyer should be able to request witness protection, if you're willing to testify against the men who murdered Esteban Ramirez."

The detective excused himself, leaving me chained to the chair. It was beginning to look like testifying was my only option. I'd recognized the bodyguard and the man with the mustache who shot at me on the boat in a few photos I found online. Their faces were still etched in my brain. Unfortunately, I also knew they weren't the guys who actually shot Esteban. I couldn't identify the guys on the hill; they were too far away. I was trying to determine how helpful I would be to the murder investigation when the unnamed detective returned.

"Your lawyer is driving here, but it will be a few hours before she arrives. We will book you in for Mr. Thompson's murder, and wait for your lawyer to arrive before notifying the Vegas PD. I have an empty cell I can move you to in the meantime." He pulled the handcuff keys from his pocket, unlocked me from the chair, and refastened the cuff on my wrist. "Follow me."

I had no choice but to follow him. He was holding my arm just above my elbow. He led me past a thick security door, down a long hallway, and into a dark, dank jail cell before removing the handcuffs. He walked away without further instructions or reassurances. The cell smelled like spoiled milk, and you could hear a muffled moaning sound from further down the hall. I spent a couple of nights in a Las Vegas holding cell as a teenager, but this felt different. I didn't feel certain I'd be released in the morning.

The cell had a narrow bench along one wall and a thin mattress on a metal frame, but I chose to pace back in forth in the tiny cramped space. I replayed every detail of the last few weeks in my mind. I re-imagined myself twirling for Esteban in the pink Prada dress, remembering how excited he was to see me in it. I thought about his impressive home and yacht, and how he was going to give me the financial freedom I craved.

Of course, that made me think about the suitcase full of money—which was now entered into evidence, never to be mine again. Esteban was dead, and there was an arrest warrant out for me in connection with his murder. I wasn't sure if I could prove my innocence or be a valuable witness against the real killers. To make matters worse, I'd just confessed to killing a man and fleeing from the scene. I was already charged with one murder.

What if they think I did the same to Esteban?

It felt like the walls were closing in on me. I wanted to scream and bang on the bars like you see prisoners do in the movies. I had no idea how long it would take for the lawyer to arrive. There was no way for me to know the current time, and the panic I felt earlier was starting to rise even more. I was gasping for a full breath and couldn't bear to be left alone with my thoughts any longer.

I paced back and forth for hours, until my legs felt too weak to continue. I had just decided to plop myself on the metal bench when I heard two people approaching. It was the guard who had brought me there, with a leggy brunette dressed in a navy-blue power suit.

"She's in there." He opened the door and motioned for the woman to go inside the cell. "I have to relock it, but I'll be standing right outside if anything happens."

His comment made me feel like a dangerous offender. I guess I was a murderer after all.

"Thank you." She gave the guard a nod of approval and then turned her attention to me. "Samantha Tilson? I'm Christine Demarais, but you can call me Chris. Donna filled me in on what happened, and I think I can help."

I had just sat down and my legs were shaking. I tried to respond, but felt paralyzed.

"I called the LVPD to find out the terms of your arrest warrant, and received some reassuring news. The warrant was issued for the theft of the briefcase and obstruction of justice. They've already caught several of the men responsible for Mr. Ramirez's murder, and are anxious to find out if you can help close their case."

I jumped from the bench, eyes wide and arms spread out in search of a celebratory hug. "Are you serious? They know I didn't kill him? I was so worried they thought I killed Esteban. I didn't know how I'd prove my innocence."

"I guess cameras at the marina captured the men shooting at you. They also captured you fleeing with the suitcase, which they suspected held a substantial amount of money, but I'm hoping we can justify why you ran. I'd like to take your full statement, explaining everything that happened before and after the murder. I'm going to work with the lawyers handling the case to see if I can get you a deal in exchange for your testimony. Are you comfortable testifying?"

"I wasn't before, but I guarantee I can do it now." What seemed impossible a few minutes ago, now didn't feel nearly as frightening.

"Let's start from the beginning. Just tell me everything you know about Esteban's connections, criminal activity, and the details of the night of his murder." Chris pulled a tape recorder out of her briefcase, turned it on, and held it within a foot of my face.

"I didn't know about Esteban's criminal activity until after his murder, but there were a few suspicious signs I should have picked up on." I took a deep breath and explained our first encounter, the diligence of his bodyguards, the man with the mustache, and then every minute of our last evening together. I told her about the killers threatening my roommate, the phone calls and texts that followed, and how I finally escaped into Canada.

"I didn't know the police had connected me to the crime until I was already in Windsor."

"Why didn't you go to the police immediately?"

"I know a lot of the Vegas PD are close friends with the local drug cartel. Almost every cop I've met was crooked, including the one who knocked up my mom. I still think they'll turn me over to the cartel once they find me."

"I'm certain they're not all corrupt, but I'll petition to keep you in Canada until the trial. We can use the Thompson murder trial as justification. What was your old cellphone number?"

"Why?"

"I'm going to get an authorization form to release your old cell phone records. It will have the threatening text and voice messages you mentioned. That will help prove why you felt the need to flee. You did get threats, correct?"

"Yes, several. Wow! That would be great." I gave her my old number, and she excused herself to prepare the necessary paperwork. I couldn't stop smiling. I had gone from imagining the worst to legitimate hope this awful mess would soon be over.

Chris came back around ten minutes later with the authorization form. I eagerly signed, and thanked her for helping. She advised me she would be gone for a few hours, but promised she'd be back before nightfall.

"I'm going to prepare your statement, request the phone records, and see if I can get you released into my custody for the night. Worst case, you may need to spend the night here. I'll do my best to quickly resolve the request for bail. Do you have access to any funds?"

"No, I was living off of the money from the briefcase?"

"It's all right. If you can get bail tonight, I'll cover it."

"Thank you! Thank you so much." I gushed, resisting the urge to hug her. The thought of spending one night in jail didn't scare me, now that there was hope I'd be out soon.

Shortly after Chris left, the guard brought me a sloppy mess of what I assumed was my dinner on a faded grey plastic tray. I picked at the stale bun and ate a few of the tasteless corn niblets to quiet the rumbling in my belly. I was desperately hungry, but couldn't stomach the sight and smell of the unidentifiable brown mound in the center of the tray.

When the young guard came back to remove the uneaten tray, he warned me that it would be the only food I would get until morning. The day had been an emotional rollercoaster already, and if recent events had taught me anything, it's that my stomach doesn't handle stress well. I decided not eating was better than spending the night in a cell with my own vomit.

Although the meeting with my new lawyer was encouraging, the loneliness of the cold, empty cell was chipping away at my newfound hope. I might not be going away for murder, but I still had to testify against some of Vegas's most dangerous men. I wouldn't be able to return and resume my life as a Vegas showgirl. After about an hour of pondering what I was going to do with my post-apocalypse life, Chris returned to break the bad news to me.

"I won't be able to get you released tonight. I've submitted your statement and requested the phone records. I'm going to stay in town tonight, and come back tomorrow morning after the judge determines your bail amount. I updated Donna on our progress, and she said everyone is sending their love and prayers. Try to get some sleep. Tomorrow will be a better day."

My head bobbed up and down repeatedly; I was too choked up to reply. Tears began to blur my vision as she walked away. That dear, sweet stranger revived my hope from earlier. Better days were on their way; all I needed to do was survive the night.

I had survived much worse. My mother was a train wreck, and I'd survived her. I was a self-destructive teenager, and I'd managed to break free from the drugs and men that tried to hold me back. There were bullets whizzing towards me, yet I had steered the ship to safety. For fuck's sake, a serial rapist and murderer had plans to bury me in his backyard, and I ended his life instead.

I am a survivor.

I had spent the last few weeks beating myself up for all the mistakes I made along the way, when the only thing that really mattered was that I lived to tell the story. There were so many times when I could have given up, but I didn't. Leaning up against the hard cement wall, staring at the steel bars that separated me from society, was the first time I felt free. I was strong, resilient, and had what it takes to start over. I could finally picture my life having a happy ending.

Unfortunately, that night wasn't the end of my struggles, or my last night in a jail cell. There were still many legal details to resolve concerning both crimes. Two countries, two murders, and two serious counts of leaving the scene of a crime and obstruction of justice. My situation was unique and complicated. It took three days before Chris could post bail, because she wanted to make sure I wouldn't be immediately extradited to the states upon my release. She made arrangements for me to go back to the shelter while the rest of my fate was being negotiated.

My cellphone records were my saving grace. Although they couldn't link the other cellphone number to anyone charged with Esteban's murder, it did prove that I ran because I feared for my life. It took several weeks, including a brief trip to Vegas so I could appear in front of a judge, before they finally worked out a plea deal.

The prosecution agreed to drop all charges against me in relation to Esteban's murder in exchange for my testimony. Esteban's murder trial wouldn't happen for a least a year. I would need that time to prepare for Richard Thompson's murder trial, so the American judge allowed me to be released into Chris's custody until it was time for me to stand in both trials. That incredible deal meant I could stay in Canada, where it was considerably safer.

Chris went above and beyond the normal duties of a lawyer. At my request, she called my grandma to assure her of my safety, and even paid for her to visit me for a few days. I tried to talk my grandma into moving to Canada, but she was a proud American who refused to live anywhere besides Vegas.

The pre-trial for Richard's murder happened faster than we were expecting. The judge was eager to dismiss the murder charges on the grounds of self-defense. He lessened the charges to leaving the scene of a crime, obstruction of justice, and manslaughter for leaving him there to die. The case went to trial eight months later, and the jury only found me guilty of obstruction of justice. I was sentenced to 90 days in jail.

I'll spare everyone the boring details of my 90 days in jail, since I spent most of my time working out while writing this book in my head. At the end of the sentence, I was in the best physical and mental shape of my life. I realized that my experiences could give hope to others, and I was determined to become like the wonderful women who welcomed me at the shelter. All the women took the time to visit me in jail, and Doris reassured me that I'd have a place to stay once I was released again.

Once I was let out of jail, I was surprised to discover that I had become a local hero. Ontario has only been home to a few serial killers and rapists, and details of the trial had flooded the airwaves. Everyone was eager to cheer for the woman who took him out. Chris gave me a collection of articles and emails praising what I had done.

Time to Testify

The trial for Esteban's murder was scheduled to begin a few weeks after I finished my jail sentence. I spent all of my free time preparing to testify against Esteban's murders. The American lawyer who was handling the case for the prosecution only came to see me once while I was in jail to discuss the trial. Thankfully, Chris volunteered to be a liaison for Esteban's trial, and had already started working with me on it when we were preparing my defense for Richard's murder.

I worked the morning shift at the diner, walked to Chris's office to go over my testimony, and then went home to help prepare dinner. After we cleaned up the kitchen, Donna would pretend to be the lawyer for the defense and cross examine me. Both women assured me that being on the stand would go well, as long as I was honest and confident.

It had been a little more than a year since I first met Esteban, and it was now time to face his murders. To say I was nervous was an understatement. I applied deodorant three times before leaving the shelter. Janice volunteered to drive Donna, Chris, and I to Toronto airport. Janice and Doris were originally planning to go with me for support, but a new woman had arrived at the shelter two days before. She had a broken arm, bruises everywhere, and was still too scared to open up to anyone. They didn't want to leave her until she'd had a chance to adjust to her new home.

Chris and Donna kept the conversation light throughout the flight, and insisted on squeezing in some fun while we were in Vegas. We were arriving Sunday afternoon, and the trial wasn't until 9:30 the following morning. They were excited to see where I used to dance, so we went to Planet Hollywood for dinner.

For a few, freeing hours, it felt like I was on vacation with close friends. We ate amazing food, laughed loudly, and gushed over the beauty and complexity of the dance routine. It was the first time either woman had been to Vegas, so we toured the nearby strip to well past 10:00 pm.

I felt proud to show off my hometown to my Canadian friends—until we returned to our room. We were sharing a room with two beds and a cot. There was a small box with an envelope sitting on top of the cot. "Samantha" was sloppily scribbled across the top in red marker. I felt certain it wasn't a gift.

"Where did that come from?" Donna asked with the same level of concern and uncertainty that was already swimming in my gut.

"No idea. Should I open it?" I posed the question to Chris, who was staring at the ominous box.

"We should probably call the police first. I'll get a hold of hotel security to see if anyone was let into our room."

"What if it's a bomb?" Donna shouted. "Should we still be in here?"

"It didn't go off when we entered the room, so it should be safe. Maybe you should take Sam back to the bar while I sort this out," Chris answered calmly.

"Absolutely not! This is here because of me, and I can't let you fight every battle on my behalf!"

Without hesitating, I firmly requested that both women step outside of the room, so I could open the box. I had to physically push Chris and Donna back through the entranceway. I quickly slammed the door shut and locked it, then slowly walked over to the cot.

I decided to remove the envelope first. I carefully peeled the tape that was holding it to the box and gently broke open the seal. The only thing inside was a picture of my grandma's trailer. Vomit rose from my belly, but I pushed it back down.

I dropped the envelope and photo on the hotel floor as I picked up the box. It felt way too light to be a bomb, so I tore off the lid and braced myself for the worst. Inside was one of grandma's lucky poker hats and a pack of long matches. My first reaction was a loud, piercing scream, which caused Chris and Donna to start pounding frantically on the door.

I dropped the box, ran to the door, and let my companions back inside.

"Are you okay?" Donna rushed to my side.

I stood there shaking, while Donna rubbed my back and Chris picked up the miscellaneous items that were scattered across the floor.

"Whose trailer is this?" Chris held the photo up in front of me. Tears filled my eyes.

"My grandma's."

"So, it's a threat. I'll contact the authorities, and your lawyer. We'll make sure she's secure until after the trial. They are just trying to scare you out of testifying. Don't let it work."

"I can't put her life in jeopardy."

"We won't. Pack up your stuff, and I'll get us moved to a different location. We have to trust the police this time. I'll do whatever I can to keep you and your grandma safe."

For a moment, it felt like my shoes were filled with cement. I would never forgive myself if something happened to my sweet, crazy grandma.

"Let's go. I'll arrange for hotel security to wait with us until the police escort arrives. They'll take your grandma somewhere safe until after the trial."

"Thank you." I shouted, as I ran to grab my belongings.

The three of us rushed down to the lobby, where we were met with the hotel manager and one security guard. Chris didn't tell them I was a witness in a murder, only that I'd received a threat against my life. Both insisted on waiting with us.

Two local officers, one DEA agent, a federal officer, the American lawyer who was representing me in the trial, and his assistant all showed up to ensure my transfer to the police station was successful. While we were driving in two armored vans to the Las Vegas Metro Police Station, another local officer, a detective, and two DEA agents were headed to my grandma's trailer to pick her up.

It was agreed that three of us and my grandma would spend the night in their custody. My testimony was expected to be over well before lunch, and they would sneak us all to a hotel in a different city immediately afterwards. My heart was beating rapidly, but I remained calm. Everything appeared to be under control.

I knew my heart wouldn't stop racing until I physically saw my grandma. I wasn't aware at the time that the group of law enforcement sent out to secure grandma was headed back empty handed. The lock was broken on her trailer door, and no one was inside.

My companions and I were escorted into the station with the federal officer in front, an officer on each side, and the DEA agent in the back. The legal assistant waited until everyone else was inside before exiting the van. He looked young and nervous, so I assumed he didn't want to be too close to a potential sniper target.

No bullets whizzed towards me this time, thank God! Upon our arrival, they put Donna with me in an interview room until they could secure a more comfortable spot. Chris stayed outside, making phone calls and planning a less-direct flight home.

The station had a nicer seating area for victims or officers when they were on their break. Sadly, it was currently in use. Someone had to tell a single mom her son was being arrested for texting and driving. He drove into a cement light pole, killing the passenger in the car: his sister.

The officer who brought us into the interrogation room explained that devastating tragedy, which had just occurred, to us. He told us his captain voluntarily accepted the heart-wrenching task, but admitted this was the first time he had to tell a mother that her daughter was dead and her son would be going to jail for it.

As bone-chilling as the tragic story was to imagine, my mind was elsewhere. I was having flashbacks to waiting inside a similar room prior to confessing the ugly mess I was in. I didn't feel nearly as safe as I should feel, surrounded by law enforcement. Donna's face couldn't hide her fear, either. She stared at the wall, clearly lost in her own panicky thoughts. I don't think either of us noticed when the officer stopped talking.

We were interrupted about ten minutes into our internal dialogues by Chris. She asked if there was any place my grandma would go in the middle of the night. The trailer was empty when they got there, and the front door was broken off the hinges.

I was trying not imagine the worst, reassuring myself that although my grandma was 72, she still stayed out past midnight if she was on a winning streak. It was possible that she was still playing poker. At my recommendation, they left two officers within sight of her trailer and then sent two other officers to her two favorite poker rooms.

After she didn't turn up at either of those games, or return to her trailer by 2:00 am, the station issued a missing person's bulletin early, due to the severity of the threat and potential danger of the murder trial. I was trying so hard to stay calm and positive, but my gut ached. I paced the floor of the tiny room for twenty minutes before they sent us to a room with a couch and several comfortable chairs. Donna plopped on the sofa, looking utterly exhausted. I continued pacing in silence. My body was tired, but my mind forced me to keep moving.

Fortunately, I only had to wait about an hour to find out she was safe from harm. In fact, she was already at another local police station. She came home from playing cards at 11:00 pm and saw her door was broken. Grandma could tell her belongings had been moved, and that her lucky hat was gone. She immediately looked for her poker hat because she had lost miserably, and blamed her bad luck on forgetting to wear it.

She waited in the police station for almost four hours before a detective would take her story. The officer who spoke with her when she first arrived brushed her off as low priority, since she was only complaining about someone stealing her hat. When a detective finally listened, he recognized her name and address as being the same as the earlier bulletin. They immediately placed her in a secure location and explained the plans for the following day.

I was disappointed that I couldn't be with her, but felt relieved that she was as safe as she could be considering the circumstances. I trusted that I would see her tomorrow after the trial. I also finally felt confident that I could testify without *succumbing to my fear.*

I was ready to rebuild a better life with my grandma that was free from all this Vegas drama. I decided I needed to ensure our safety and future beyond tomorrow, so I asked a nearby officer to request a visit with my lawyer before the trial. Once I knew what I had to do, I was finally able to sit down and relax a bit. I never fell asleep, but I remained calm. I felt relief knowing that the fear and uncertainty from the last year would be behind me in a matter of hours.

The American lawyer representing me in court went home for a nap, but Chris returned to our room just after 6:00 am. I knew she didn't leave the station, and could tell she hadn't slept, either. I felt bad that I was going to make some demands so late in the game—but I'm a survivor, and I had to do what was best for me.

"Chris, I need to add a couple conditions to my testifying today."

"Still scared?'

"Very, and I need to make sure my grandma and I have a future."

"I understand, and hopefully can get a few reasonable requests approved by the prosecution."

"I need you to sponsor my grandma and me for our Canadian citizenship."

"I would be happy to do that."

"I also want help securely relocating my grandma and me to Burlington."

"That's a reasonable request that we would have done for her regardless."

"I would appreciate selling her trailer and getting her one near the shelter. I plan on volunteering there."

"That shouldn't be a problem, either."

"I want to repay you one day, but in the meantime, I'd like to volunteer for you as well."

"That's definitely doable!" Chris said enthusiastically, followed by a firm hug. Donna was half asleep, curled up in a ball on the couch. When she saw us hugging, she jumped up and joined in.

"Anything else, Sam?" Chris asked after we pulled apart.

"Nope! I already have everything else I need."

"Okay. I need to make a few phone calls to take care of these little details, and I'll be back in hour to go over your testimony one more time. I'm so proud of you, Sam!" Chris blew me a kiss before heading back into the hallway.

I was proud of me, too. When I was faced with danger, I stayed calm and got through it. I knew the trial would be just as successful. I encouraged Donna to go back to sleep. I sat back down and went over the details of that night on the boat. Although it happened only about a year ago, it felt like a previous life.

When it was finally time to testify, I walked into the courtroom looking and feeling like an upstanding member of society. I held my head high; I spoke clearly when questioned, and gave every detail I could remember. The cross examination by the defense wasn't easy, but I didn't let my past indiscretions discredit me, even when they relentlessly questioned my fleeing with the briefcase of cash.

"You ran away with over three hundred thousand in cash. How do we know you didn't kill him, so you could steal the money?"

"I was falling in love with Esteban. He was spoiling and flattering me. He was everything I thought I wanted."

"Thought you wanted? When did you decide you no longer wanted Mr. Ramirez?" The defense attorney smugly replied.

"I still want the Esteban I thought he was, before I Googled him after his murder. Turns out I didn't know the real Esteban. Luckily, I got to know the real me since then, and I don't need a rich man coming to my rescue. I can save myself!" I stated proudly.

The defense attorney was not expecting my reply and took a minute or two to respond. I sat there calm and confident while I waited for the drilling to continue.

"In your earlier testimony, you mentioned you had your suspicions due to some of the activity you witnessed. Why didn't you Google him then?"

"He swept me off my feet. He showered me with expensive gifts, took me out to fancy dinners, and for evening cruises on his massive yacht. I didn't want to break the fairytale illusion I was living."

"So you were using him for his money, and then took off with three hundred thousand dollars? Did you find the money and figure this was your chance to have everything you ever wanted without the potentially dangerous relationship?" The intimidating lawyer continued.

"Everything I wanted at that moment was Esteban. He made me feel special. The sex was amazing; we were insatiable. I melted around him. When I heard the gunshot, I felt my heart drop. I didn't want to believe he was dead." Genuine tears rolled down my cheeks. I had been falling in love with Esteban, and still couldn't quite believe he was gone.

"Yet you were calm enough to steer a massive yacht, while you were apparently being shot at?"

"I saw the men running towards me. I watched them draw their guns. My survival instinct kicked in. I've steered big boats before, and knew it was my only chance of escaping with my life."

"Isn't that the same reason you gave for killing that man in Canada a week later?"

My stomach muscles clenched to stop me from trembling. I knew I needed to calmly explain exactly what happened, and not get overly emotional. We had practiced what I would say if the defense discovered what happened to Rick. They would want me to get frazzled and defensive so I lost credibility. I was prepared to get through it.

"That man had several bodies buried in his backyard. He drugged me, and intended to rape and kill me. He had done the same to several other women. I was tried for the crime, and only convicted of obstruction of justice. I am a hero for what I did. Because of my actions, that murdering rapist can't hurt anyone else." I forced a sincere, closed-lip smile at the end.

The defense backed off and declared they had no more questions. I exhaled and went back to my seat. A few minutes later, Chris said she was stepping into the hall, and for us to follow separately a few minutes after. Donna went second; after waiting a whole 30 seconds, I followed her almost immediately. Chris was waiting for us just outside the door.

"You did great, Sam! I'm so proud of you." Of course, this was followed by a group hug before Chris got back down to business.

"We have an unmarked police car outside with your grandma in it. We're going to be dropped off at a bus station, take an hour bus trip, and then a short cab ride to a hotel that has already been secured. We'll sleep there until tomorrow. Sleep needs to be our first priority."

We eagerly agreed, and I raced outside to see grandma. We hugged each other the best we could in the backseat of the car, before riding hand in hand to the bus stop. We spent the entire journey catching up on everything that had happened. She was so proud of me for testifying.

Over the course of the trip, Chris explained the rest of our convoluted escape back into Canada. She'd arranged for us to take a plane to New York, then a train to Michigan, followed by an unmarked police escort crossing the border into Sarnia. From there, it was a rental car to Toronto and the Go Train into Burlington. My grandma's new trailer was waiting for us when we got back.

The American lawyer handling the case called Chris a few weeks later. The verdict didn't take long; all five men were charged with murder. The four who didn't pull the trigger received 25 years. The guy who shot Esteban received life without parole. Justice was served, and I was a part of it.

I was so grateful to Chris, Donna, Doris, and all the women I'd met that I kept all of my promises. I worked at the diner five days a week, donating half of my wage to the shelter. I volunteered at the law office, handling administrative functions like filing and typing. Chris would also let me research cases when she was overloaded. I learned so much, including how to properly type with two hands. My new skill became very useful when I decided to share the story I wrote in my head during my three months in jail.

I used to wish for a Prince Charming to rush in and save me. My life is now better than I ever imagined, and it wasn't a man that created this beautiful new world; *I* did. When the worst of the world did its best to tear me down, I became my own hero.

Your Own Hero

By Jenn Sadai

When the world destroys your heart
And it feels like everything's falling apart.
Trust you have the strength to rise again.
Have faith that this won't be the end.

When fear runs wild and tomorrow's uncertain.
It's hard to breathe and it won't stop hurting.
Dig down deep and cling to any ounce of hope.
Just like every time before, you'll find a way to cope.

Rain and thunder may beat down on you today.
And you don't know if tomorrow will start a better way.
Brace yourself to overcome the challenge in front of you.
Look within and you'll see what you need to do.

Every life will have hardships that try to hold you down.
We must believe we have what it takes to go another round.
It's within us to pick ourselves up, no matter how low.
We need to step up and become our very own hero.

About the Author

Jenn Sadai is on a mission to support and inspire women. Her first book, *Dark Confessions of an Extraordinary, Ordinary Woman* delves into the dark consequences of domestic violence, drug use, and depression. Jenn shares her experiences in the hope it will help others with similar struggles. Her second book, *Dirty Secrets of the World's Worst Employee*, follows Jenn's crooked career path and the obstacles she overcame while discovering her true calling. Her professional journey tackles critical issues such as gender equality, sexual harassment and workplace bullying.

Cottage Cheese Thighs is the third book in her "Self-esteem Series." It dissects and rejects society's perception of how a woman should look, while teaching the reader how to love their own body, flaws and all. *Her Own Hero* is Jenn's first attempt at fiction, but she promises it won't be her last.

Jenn Sadai is a proud Canadian, born in Windsor, Ontario, where she resides with her heroic husband, super stepchildren, and two lovable labs. You can reach Jenn through the various social media links on her website, www.jennsadai.com.

Coming Soon

Jenn Sadai plans on publishing her fourth self-help memoir, *No Kids Required*, early in 2018. This book will be a collaboration of different women's experiences with their decision not to have children. She is also working on another fictional story based on Katelyn from *Her Own Hero*.

CPSIA information can be obtained
at www.ICGtesting.com
Printed in the USA
LVHW03s1826190718
584343LV00001B/160/P